SLIPPING THROUGH THE NET

JENNIFER ASHCROFT

Chapters

Foreword

Throughout history England has been held as the land of plenty and the reason why thousands flocked to its shores. It's a sanctuary in the eyes of the world, with an endless image of security and stability.

A picture of fifty shades of green comes to mind, where the rolling hills and fields stand in peaceful harmony. And at the end of every wet day the sun breaks through and there's a rainbow where a pot of gold awaits. That's the image England portrays to the rest of the world and for some it is indeed a wonderful place. But for many it is not what it seems.

For two thousand years Christianity held families together in England's communities. But in the twentieth century we started to stop needing that 'old fashioned' system of faith that still exists in other countries today. Family has always been the bedrock of society and the good rules of it used to be encouraged by the church. As the churches influence started to cease more families failed and the society sickened and withered. Secularism filled the gap with its safety net of 'the Social Services' who were, and still are, supposed to catch and protect the children and youths of the failing families.

The English are seen as privileged and spoilt and little is heard about those who dropped through that 'safety net.' Maybe because they either didn't survive to tell the tale or they lacked education and were unable to put the words together because of their disrupted journey during school years. Or they blotted the memories out because they were too painful. Or they were deliberately discouraged from disclosing their story. Or they thought no one cared to hear.

The most beautiful pieces of art and literature humanity has ever produced have largely been the work of people who couldn't find anyone in the vicinity to talk to.

If you come to England looking for that pot of gold at the end of the rainbow, beware - rainbows don't really exist, they're just illusions. And you might find yourself looking for that pot of gold for the rest of your miserable life. If you're born English you are likely on a more perilous journey than you realise. Some will thrive, most will be alright and some will be grappling to survive and slipping through the net.

This is a true story.

Some of the names have been changed.

Prologue

I felt almost ready to faint. So vivid was my sense of crises. At any other moment of my life, prior to that day, I would have refused such company. But at sixteen and traumatized by recent events my only plan was walking the streets to try and avoid my misery. In reduced circumstances you have to convince yourself to remain alive. In reduced circumstances you have to trick yourself to stay sane. But evil looks for such innocence and vulnerability. Evil waits for the girls that are easy prey. Evil came too close that day.

CHAPTER 1

Hollymount

The city of Worcester wasn't famous for much in particular. There were only two things as far as I knew. One thing was the world famous Worcester Porcelain that apparently churned out some of the most exquisitely decorated fine bone china. I say 'apparently exquisite' as I never went inside the porcelain factory in the city centre. My family never owned any of their ornaments or crockery, so we certainly were not experts on the subject.

The other claim to fame was Lee and Perrin, the Worcestershire sauce factory that was located on our side of town. I never saw anyone go in or out of that place and the huge gates were always locked when I passed by. It was a mysterious place like Charlie's Chocolate Factory. I imagined the Oompa Loompas beavering away inside. The smell of tomato and anchovies and the other secret ingredients lingered in the streets of Worcester, like the permanent backdrop to my invisible story.

Our street was unusually named Hollymount. Not Hollymount street or Hollymount Road, it was just Hollymount. Our three bedroomed, detached house had a large front and back garden and separate garage. It stood in a row of privately owned houses, the only row of private houses that ran through the middle of a huge council estate. 'Snobs!' That's what the council kids used to call the kids from Hollymount but I took it as a joke. I had a lot of good friends from the surrounding estate as well as from my street.

Our house had a huge lime coloured living room, separate dining room and a large kitchen diner. I was accustomed to having my own bedroom which featured a magnificent scene through the window. A breath-taking view stretched over the city of Worcester, where the cathedral dominated the skyline and the Malvern Hills framed the horizon. We lived right in the middle of our street and directly opposite was a convenience store/sweet shop, called Box's shop. For a child in the 1970's, it was an agreeable situation.

During the week our mum took care of my older sister Carol and I while our dad was out working at Worcester general post office in the city centre. It was usual for fathers to go out to work while mothers stayed home to take care of the house. The majority of families in the street had the same set up. This meant that after completing some household chores, Mum had plenty of other women to natter with. Their husbands were also at work and the children played out in their gardens and out on the street together.

Our family of four was particularly musical. Mum and Dad could both play the upright piano situated in our dining room. We all sang well and my sister and I both learned to read music before even entering primary school at the age of five. We often sang together in a family circle in the car on journeys and short trips. But it was Dad who really had a talent for music. He was a semi-professional trumpet player and he could also play just about any other instrument he wished to attempt. He regularly treated himself to a new 'second hand' instrument and then would practise and practise until he could at least play to a reasonable level.

My primary school was at the end of our street and I knew just about every child that attended and recognised most people in the neighbourhood. I was content and as is usual for us humans, I took for granted the security and stability of my environment.

Next door to us lived the only family I ever knew that actually owned some items from Worcester Porcelain. In fact the Smiths had a whole cabinet of the crockery as ornaments. They didn't even use it. Apparently it was just for looking at. Their only daughter Sarah was my best friend automatically as our mothers' coffee mornings would place us in each other's company on a regular basis. Her parents had more money than most in the area and as a consequence Sarah was pampered with just about whatever she wanted. Her mother would often curl Sarah's blonde hair every morning before school and have her dressed in the smartest of outfits. They didn't concern themselves with the fact that the area had a fair amount of poverty stricken families. Some referred to Sarah as spoilt. She certainly had an air of superiority about her, even as a young child, that rubbed others up the wrong way including me. Our friendship was more out of convenience than caring. We went to primary school together and often played out together on our yellow garden swing or Sarah's flower filled back garden.

Sarah's mother did her daughter no favours although every move she made was with the opposite intention. Annually our primary school insisted on us all competing in an 'Easter basket competition' where we were to provide our own materials and produce an artistically decorated egg filled basket, over the course of a weekend. There was always a prize for the most beautiful presentation and the entries would finally finish up as charity at a local old folks' home. The effort put in by me and the other children in my class, with our old fruit boxes and crepe paper, would take hours of our time. Our excitement on carrying our rough designs in on the Monday morning in anticipation of being called out 'the Winner!'

in front of the entire school was insurmountable. But by the age of seven or eight I had already learned that there was only ever going to be one winner for this competition. Sarah's mum was a genius when it came to cake decoration and even made wedding cakes as a hobby. She had an eye for attention to detail and the means to afford such beautiful craftwork accessories.

My bashed up monstrosity consisted of some screwed up hard toilet paper with three chicken eggs, stuck with sticky tape inside a battered old fruit box. With the box on one arm I checked myself in the downstairs hall mirror. I was tiny and skinny with reddish brown hair kept short around shoulder length and a bright green ribbon tied in a bow.

'It brings the green out ya eyes' Mum said.

'Ye I likes it Mum - I'm going ta school now - t'ra'

As usual I called for Sarah on my way. Her back kitchen door was open and her spectacular Easter basket was displayed on the table. A real wicker basket dotted with tiny yellow fluffy chicken stickers and silky blue ribbons. It was filled with soft white cotton and twelve chicken eggs neatly placed as if measured by ruler. Delicate pastel coloured flowers hand-made out of icing sugar added to the sparkling see through paper. Sarah's entry to the competition was a true work of art. If the other mums had helped their children they could not have competed with that level of expertise. Anyway it was meant to be the child's work and so it was claimed that Sarah had made it herself and so year on year she won the prizes. But as a consequence the school children felt cheated and she was always short on friends.

In the summer of 1973 when I was eight years old, a new family moved into our street. Their detached house was next door to us on the opposite side to Sarah. The Macks were a family of six. As well as the parents, there was a fourteen year old boy and three younger girls aged thirteen, eleven and seven. My sister and I welcomed them to the street and almost instantly became great friends with them. When not at school we were usually out playing together. We played cricket in their back garden, football in the street and chase over the park. We ran around for hours on hot summer days and cold rainy days.

I became great friends with the youngest from this family. Lisa Mack was a pretty little thing with long, straight mousy brown hair. She was kind, funny and innocent and even though she was nearly two years younger than myself, we got along really well and seemed to have similar interests in common. We had the love of musical theatre and animals. We both had a mixed breed dog and we would sometimes walk them together for miles across the city, even at such a young age. We would walk along the river Severn or play in the grounds of the cathedral. We knew we had to stick together and not to talk to strangers. We were always together, either alone chatting or playing out with all the other siblings and children from the street. Our love of singing and dancing would often cause us to spend hours in front of a mirror whilst holding onto a hairbrush as a pretend microphone. Many hours were spent bouncing on our space-hoppers until they'd been punctured and repaired too many times to fix. Then we might strip down to our underwear and pretend to be gymnasts or dancers for the day.

If Lisa and I were out on the street then Sarah would be free to join in our games along with the other children. But she was generally not invited to play with us when we were just an intimate two as three was always a crowd. We tended to avoid her and happy with our own company Lisa became my faithful best friend.

Lisa was not at all spoilt. Being the fourth child, material objects had to go around further in her house. We were both the youngest child of our families and that meant we would naturally receive older sister's clothes handed down to us when they no longer fitted them. These 'hand me downs' were always gratefully received and we both looked upon the passing over of the clothing as an exciting occasion.

All the kids in the street were a little wary of Lisa's mother. In the early days Lisa warned me that her mum had a bad temper and so we generally kept out of her way. There may have been issues going on in their house that I never knew about and what happened behind their closed doors was best left there. I rarely spoke about private things that happened at home and I wouldn't expect Lisa to tell me much either. We heard that discussing family business with non-family members was like washing your dirty clothes in public and we wouldn't want to do that. So instead we spent our time practising gymnastics, walking our dogs, playing on our bikes, singing or playing out on the street with other local children. If we became hungry we would sneak into either Lisa's or my kitchen and make a sugar sandwich or grab a piece of bread and dripping.

On Fridays, after school, Lisa and I got two pence each from our mothers and we would spend it at Box's shop. We couldn't wait to chew on the bubble wrapped candy. Sometimes we would bump into Sarah in the shop and she would have five pence or even ten pence to spend. It wasn't that my mum was much poorer than Sarah's mum, she just deemed certain things unnecessary and sweets was one of them. Regular square meals were cooked at home and puddings were served after dinner sometimes, so there was really no need for more sugar to be consumed. But Lisa and I nagged our mums for another penny or two 'like Sarah had!' Mum said I shouldn't be jealous of Sarah as she would be fat one day. But as I had been teased for being underweight for most of my young life the concept of 'fat' failed as a deterrent, in fact I may well have envied Sarah's slightly chubby physique. Either way I had no chance of obtaining any further pennies from Mum. She had been a poor farmer's daughter and was unimpressed by the superficialities of life. She had learned the benefits of being frugal. Luckily Lisa sometimes managed to squeeze an extra penny or two from Mrs Mack and she shared any extra sweets with me.

It was a happy street to grow up in and to the outside world we must have looked like the perfect, happy family. We had a car and always had a family holiday every year either camping in Wales or to a holiday camp. In those days not everyone had such privileges. Some of my school friends were so poor that they'd never even been able to afford to go outside of Worcester for even a day trip. Some of them had never even climbed the Malvern Hills even though their beauty dominated our city and were only ten miles away on the other side of town. I suppose ten miles is quite a distance if you don't own a car and have more necessary things to spend money on than public transport for day trips.

As an underweight child I often tolerated ill health, 'failure to thrive' they called it. I generally caught every cough and cold that was going around and by the age of eight I had already suffered pneumonia and several other serious chest infections and childhood illnesses. As a result of all this sickliness I had become rather clingy to my mum. She was my anchor.

CHAPTER 2

Ballerina

Dad played and sang in a dance-band and we often went along with him to the working men's clubs where he performed on weekends. I enjoyed these nights out immensely. The band would play and all the adults would dance the Fox-Trot and other ballroom style dances in the packed, cigarette smoke filled dance hall. When the band took a break, Dad would come and sit with us at our table while the bingo was on. Usually there would be a raffle too. One time the main raffle prize was a giant teddy-bear! All the prizes had been put up on the stage while the band was taking their break and Mum suggested I go take a look at the items we might win. I stood and gazed up at the huge teddy. It was bigger than me. I returned to the table with tears in my eyes and Mum was perplexed. I explained that the giant teddy was in a huge plastic bag and therefore he couldn't breathe! Mum smiled sweetly to herself and instantly got up out of her seat. She walked across the smoke filled room and clambered up on to the stage. People were looking over now, wondering what she was doing. I stood at the bottom of the stage while Mum ripped a tiny hole in the plastic bag, next to the teddy-bear's mouth.

'There you go Jen, he can breathe now,' she announced. I felt relieved and I didn't even mind too much when we didn't win anything in the raffle.

I had my own favourite teddy-bear anyway. His name was Craig and I sometimes took him to one of the clubs with us. He was only small but very cute I thought. I had played with him for several years and one time we were at one of the clubs when Craig's worn-out nose fell off. I was very upset but Mum soon calmed me down by saying she would sew another nose on when we got home.

Next morning Mum was busy with the black cotton and a needle. She sewed a new nose for Craig so well, it was even better than the original nose. She really was the best mum.

My relationship with Dad was different. It wasn't that he preferred Carol but it just seemed that he was incapable of loving us both at the same time. He created an atmosphere with a certain kind of military order. A pecking order where there was clearly one leader and his chosen lieutenant. My position as the youngest, most sensitive and weakest member of the company was usually at the bottom. He seemed to thoroughly enjoy setting us up against each other. My sister, being three years older, may have learnt sooner than I on how to handle him and became prepared to do whatever she could to get on his good side. Carol would generally laugh off his negative remarks while I would take them to heart. As I became upset he would encourage Carol to team up with him by referring to her as 'Daddy's girl' this meant I was out of the circle. Then he would encourage her to taunt me with words such as skinny ribs, weakling and 'the Ugly Sister' until I would eventually cry.

As well as the verbal taunts there was also a continuous threat of what I can only describe as physical overpowering. No hitting or punching as such, more like putting us in stress-positions. Being at the bottom of the pecking order I took the brunt of this procedure most often. I would wriggle and squirm with all my might to try to escape his obvious strength as he held me with my arms up behind my back or pinned me down to the ground. It was very uncomfortable and I would be in tears pleading with him to release me until I had reached a blind-panic and eventually he would let go. Then a little more name calling and usually it was done for a day or two. This kind of thing was normally referred to as teasing or joking. When I complained to Mum, who was always in a different room when this activity took place, she would just brush it off and assume I was being over sensitive or tell me I should try to laugh it off as Carol generally did.

During Dad's formative years, he had been in the armed forces and perhaps this had affected his style of parenting. I was continually confused by it and not sure what it was all about or what it meant or why he did it or even if I was just being over-sensitive. Perhaps if we'd been sons rather than daughters we may have appreciated this 'rough play' but I most certainly didn't understand it and didn't like it at all.

I often felt sure that for some reason my dad disliked me and I racked my brains to consider why. I thought that maybe he was disappointed with having two daughters and perhaps would have preferred the second one to have been a boy at least. Mum told me that when she'd been expecting me she was planning on calling me Robert as she thought or hoped I was a boy. She didn't seem disappointed with having a second girl though but maybe Dad was. Or was he angry with me for being a sickly child? I even considered that he was not my real father. I never had any evidence for this consideration other than his manner towards me so the unanswered question was inevitably perplexing.

Dad was tall and handsome with dark brown hair and strikingly green eyes and I had inherited his green eyes, although not so strikingly, so I figured

I must be his. Mum had ginger hair and brown eyes and I had reddish brown hair which I concluded was a mixture from the both of them. Carol had brown eyes more like Mum's and dark hair more like Dad's. This was more than enough evidence to convince me that we were both products of them.

Sometimes our dad would terrorise my sister and I by chasing us around with a live spider or a giant, fluttering black moth in his hand. Or, if we were out, for example walking over a bridge, he might pick one of us up and dangle us by our ankles over a height or the river. Obviously he knew that he was strong enough and would not let us drop but we didn't know that and were petrified. This was carried out in full view of passers-by. In fact Dad actively sort out to create a scene by putting on a performance. The centre of attention was a comfortable place for him and the awkwardness of people's responses seemed to fulfil some of his needs. Some people would act like they hadn't noticed, some would laugh or smile and some would look horrified but no one ever intervened. Carol and I both got to a point where we would anticipate terror and panic in advance of the potential threat. These kinds of activities were always referred to as 'teasing' and if we became upset, as I usually did, we would then be criticised and humiliated for being whingers. Carol generally looked like she was coping with all of this better than me. She seemed to get in his good books more often than I did by laughing when faced with the fear. But I later realised that this incessant laughing was really hysteria.

Although the situation with my dad regularly upset me it was still normality. I had never known anything different. I just needed to try harder to avoid being alone with the two of them. But it is strange how little children are so loving and forgiving and they soon forget and drop the guard. The repeated set of scenarios would continue.

Always underweight, I started to eat less and less. I don't know why exactly, perhaps to feel some control over something or maybe I was just too busy and found sitting down to dinner uninteresting. Mum worried about me, she knew my relationships with my dad and sister, were not right. But what could she do but try to keep an eye on me and love me more? This drove a wedge of jealousy between my sister and I and my dad sometimes appeared to despise me for it.

I never understood why my dad behaved this way towards me in particular. It may have been pure entertainment for him. I never blamed my sister for it; after all, if she didn't side with him he may well have turned on her more often. So she needed to look after her own interests.

On occasion I was the favourite and Carol would take the ridicule which meant I was 'Daddy's girl' but that situation felt almost as bad and I would sympathise with Carol as I knew exactly how she was feeling. Although I had to act as though I didn't care and take his side or he could turn against me again. It was really a no-win situation. Strangely, either way, Carol and I still idolised him as girls are supposed to idolise their fathers. A little kindness from him or a present and he was instantly our hero again. When he played the trumpet and was lead singer in the dance-band, my mother, my sister and I were always insanely proud of him.

My lack of nutrition manifested in my ill health. At the age of nine a simple cold became influenza and rapidly moved on to a second bout of pneumonia. Mum was constantly by my side and recognised the signs from a previous episode. She acted fast and within no time I was referred to the hospital for treatment. I had several courses of antibiotics but my right lung was blocked with the illness. I coughed repeatedly until I was too tired to cough anymore. That's when I really took a turn for the worse. I'd been absent from school for eight weeks and the headmaster held a special assembly in my absence where the whole school prayed for me. There was a chance I might not pull through the illness and my school friends were being prepared for the worst.

A turning point came one day when I lay down on the settee and watched an old film on television that changed my outlook on life. It was a musical about the life of Hans Christian Andersen. The story of a Cobbler who made beautiful satin pointe shoes, in a variety of pastel colours, for a famous Ballerina. I was mesmerised by the ballet scenes and I wearily asked Mum to let me attend ballet classes.

'You'll have ta be very healthy and strong to be a ballet dancer!' Mum said. I was inspired to be so.

Perhaps it was a near-death experience. Maybe I was hyper sensitive at the time of watching this film. I don't know but a strong ambition overcame me and a desire not only to survive this illness but a determination to make it and to become a professional ballet dancer.

With this desire in mind I gradually recovered from my illness. Mum endeavoured, as promised, to find ballet classes for me. It took three attempts over three consecutive Saturdays. The first time we went into town we couldn't find the dance studios that Mum had heard about. The second time we found a different dance studio that only had ballroom and tap dancing lessons. Mum asked if I might prefer one of these options instead but I was adamant I wanted to do ballet. On the third attempt we located the studios that we'd searched for on the first occasion.

From the moment I walked in to Fletcher's dance studios, I loved it. On the ground floor was a huge ballroom with an electric disco ball hanging in the middle of the ceiling. Mum asked in there if this was the place where they did ballet lessons and we were told it was not and directed upstairs. As we got nearer to the top of the stairs I could smell polished wood and I could hear a piano playing classical music. Mum and I tried to peep through a crack in the door of the dance studio. Not a lot could be seen so we waited for the class to end so that we could speak to the ballet mistress.

Suddenly the piano stopped playing and a flurry of small children came running out like a cloud of pink candy floss. The teacher peered at us and then ushered us in to the mirrored studio. Her name was Barbara. She styled her jet black hair in a short, sharply cut bob and wore a material, wide patterned headband across the top of her head. She wore thick black eye makeup like she was prepared for the stage and she held a cigarette in a long cigarette-holder that she waved about while she explained everything to Mum. I was fascinated by her. She had a strict air but at the same time she seemed fair. She had a good look at me then lifted my arms and touched my back and neck. Then she asked me a few questions about myself. Next thing she offered for me to start classes the following week! I would soon require a list of items that we could purchase from the specialist dance shop in Malvern.

'You sure you still wanna do ballet?' You've not

gone off the idea?' Mum checked.

'Yes Mum, I can't wait!' I tried to contain my excitement.

Just two train stops and we were in the magnificent hills of Malvern. We came out of the train station and walked up a steep incline as Barbara had directed and there it was - the best shop I'd ever seen. I stood peering through the window, whist holding hands with my mum, amazed at the array of beautiful ballet dresses, leotards and pink pointe shoes on display. In the centre of the window display was a porcelain figurine of a little girl in a yellow tutu,

'Look Mum, look at that little statue' I said with almost uncontrolled excitement.

'That looks like Worcester porcelain's figurine of Tuesday's child,' Mum explained. 'Monday's child is fair of face and Tuesday's child is full of grace, you know graceful like a ballerina. You were born on a Tuesday! Mum continued without taking a breath, 'and you are full of grace!'

'Oh was I Mum? I really likes that statue - it would look nice in me bedroom! I hinted.

'Well I doubt it's for sale, it's just part of the display, and anyway we have too many other things to pay for today.' Mum said.

Our reflections looked back at us from the freshly cleaned windows and I moved a little to level up so as to make myself look like I was wearing one of the tutus. My eyes must have sparkled with pure delight as we entered the shop. Mum had been given a list of all the things that I needed. A pale blue regulation leotard with a separate blue elastic belt, pale pink tights with a seam up the back, a pink hair band and soft pink satin ballet shoes with satin ribbons that needed to be sewn on. It was the best day of my life! So far.

Armed with my dance kit, the following Saturday I started grade-one ballet. I noticed immediately that the other girls didn't have a Worcester accent. All of them came from either the Grammar school or the private school and had suitable private school accents. They showed kindness in their curiosity as they gathered around me.

'May I ask what your name is?' One of the girls enquired.

'Yeah it's Jennifer but me friends calls me Jenny.' All eyes were on me. 'I feels a bit hot in ere. Can we open a winda?' Their interest in me was a little overwhelming and I was getting up a sweat already.

'Oh wow, do you really say it like that?! Do you really say winda instead of window? The same girl asked but not in a mean way. The private school was boarding and several of the girls had clearly never been exposed to us locals or the Worcester accent.

I hadn't realised I had an accent until then. I was clearly a bit of a novelty at ballet class. Being shy anyway I hardly spoke at all right from the offset and if Barbara asked me a direct question I would try to speak with a posh accent like the other girls did. Even though I was a little stifled by myself I still really enjoyed the regularity of the lessons and the regimented class seemed to have a calming effect on me.

Up until I started ballet I had not been allowed to go far from Hollymount on my own. A fifteen year old girl called Carol-Ann Cooper had recently disappeared. She'd lived in a Worcester children's home and attended my sister Carol's school. That was the girl's senior school on the other side of town. She was a school-year older than Carol and so they did not know each other well. Carol-Ann had spent one weekend staying with her Grandma and had gone to the cinema in the city centre. She'd not been seen since and the whole of Worcester was at a loss to understand what had happened to her. Her black and white photograph was in every shop window including Box's. A pretty girl's picture with the wording 'Have you seen Carol-Ann Cooper?' Where had she gone - no one knew. Parents were concerned but that didn't prevent them from letting their children have the freedom to continue playing outside. We were just told to 'be careful' whatever that meant. Anyway the general consensus was that Carol-Ann had been so unhappy living in a children's home that she'd run away with a boyfriend. We didn't even know if she had a boyfriend but this scenario fitted people's logic and was a suitably convenient explanation for her disappearance. I was still allowed to go out and about with Lisa but we knew that we must always stay together.

For the first few weeks Mum accompanied me to ballet class. She would wait outside Fletcher's until my lesson was finished and then we would walk together to the end of the road to a café called the Miramar which was next door to the cinema where Carol-Ann had last been seen. There I would grab a high chrome stool, with a red faux-leather seat, up at the bar. Perched on the stool I would have a soft cheese roll and a strawberry milk shake in a tall glass with a stripy red and white paper straw. I didn't think life could get much better than that!

After a few weeks I was deemed sensible enough to get to and from my ballet lessons by myself. I knew I was not to talk to strangers. I imagined a middle aged man most likely wearing a brown suit, with a beard and perhaps a knitted brown tie. He would offer me sweets as a trick to grab me and I was to say 'no' and keep moving to get away from him. I was well prepared for this scenario.

I was a quiet child and my school reports always read that I was too timid. But academically I did well at primary school and I adored ballet class.

Even though I had missed several weeks from school, due to ill-health, I was still well ahead of most of my peers. Schools reports ranked us in order of ability for maths and English and I constantly came first, just ahead of Sarah. And my dance teacher saw that I had a gift and a passion for the theatre and a great love of everything ballet.

Dad had plenty of classical music albums. I knew for sure Tchaikovsky's 'Swan Lake' was a ballet as there was a picture like a painting of ballet dancers on the cover of the album. I wasn't sure about the other records so I repeated Swan Lake over and over. I must have played the whole album a hundred times over. I didn't know the story of Swan Lake but I had in my mind a picture of Giselle as I choreographed myself in the Prima Ballerina role and the Corps de ballet all at the same time. The dark green, leather look, settee and arm chairs would be pushed back in the living room to make as big a space as possible, my stage, and behind the old settee I would wait in the imaginary wings for the overture to finish. Undisturbed I would continue the day like that - lost in a fantasy.

When I was not practising ballet or out with Lisa, I could be found with my pets. I had a light-brown coloured dog called Sandy; she was a crazy, lovable mixture of Labrador and a variety of other breeds. I loved her and she adored me. She would follow me to the park and go on the slide with me. She even sat on the roundabout while it was turning. Some days I would actively encourage her to follow me to school and she would get over-excited in the playground jumping and barking at all the children until a teacher would find out who owned her and I would be told to 'take that dog back home!'

I also had a lovely black, fluffy, half Persian cat called Fred. He was fiercely independent but at the same time had the loveliest nature. Fred was a year or two younger than me; my very first memory is the day a tiny fluffy black ball in a basket came to our house, so I had had him nearly all my life. He had been pulled and prodded by me during my toddler years but he had never shown his claws. He was a special cat. I also had a young black and white rabbit called Flynn that we kept housed in a hutch in the garden. So I was really spoiled for pets and I loved them all. Every lunch time I would pop back home from primary school to feed them and take Sandy for a walk around the block.

These were the happy days, the days of the long hot summer days. The Best Days of our lives.

CHAPTER 3

The Back Room

My single, pink bedroom was at the front of the house. It was the smallest of the three bedrooms but it had a spectacular view over the City of Worcester with the Cathedral rising up in the centre and the Malvern Hills framing the scene. Carol, being the older sister, had the larger room at the back of the house. Although hers was double in size, I was content with my little pink room.

One day, when I was aged ten, our parents upgraded the old black and white television to a modern colour set. Carol had the old set in her bedroom with a coat hanger for an aerial and a terribly hazy picture. She persuaded me to have my things moved into her bedroom so as we could share and watch television together. We'd never shared a bedroom before. The Mack girls shared a bedroom and the thought of it sounded like fun. We would have the luxury of being able to watch television from our beds as well. I was honoured that my big sister even wanted to share with me and eagerly went along in agreement as Carol got Dad to move my bedroom furniture into her room. It was all very exciting and for a few nights I felt like I was in a luxurious hotel, watching the crackly television picture from our two single beds whilst chatting with my big sister.

'Top of the Pops' was our favourite television pro-gram. It broadcast all the latest pop stars. We were ready to watch every Thursday at seven-thirty in the evening. We never missed it but as the picture was so poor in our shared bedroom we watched it downstairs on the new colour television set. I was taken-in by a performer who sat playing the piano. He looked like an ordinary guy but he sang with such sincerity the saddest of songs about a lady called Mandy. He looked directly into the camera with tears in his eyes as he called out these tragic words.

'Well you came and you gave without taking'

'But I sent you away, oh Mandy'

'And you kissed me and stopped me from shaking'

'And I need you today oh Mandy'

I felt sure the singer was terribly heartbroken and as I liked the song I decided that I would help him in the only way I could. I decided to raid my pig-gybank and see if I had enough money to buy this poor soul's record. I felt bad for him and this act of charity would make me feel a little better.

At the end of his performance I took a note of his name and a couple of days later I purchased his single 'Mandy' which I changed when I sang it to 'Sandy' - my dog's name. That was the first record I ever bought. I had no idea that Barry Manilow wasn't some poor heartbroken soul but in fact a hugely successful international mega star. There was no Mandy in his life and therefore he was not pining for her. It was just one of the songs from one of his many multi-platinum albums.

Less than a week had passed since my stuff had been moved in with Carol and I returned home one day after playing out on the street with Lisa. As I entered the house I heard rummaging around coming from upstairs and then silence. I ran up the stairs and instantly noticed all of Carol's furniture was now in my little pink bedroom at the front of the house and she was busy putting finishing touches on making my room just as she wanted. She had apparently decided she didn't want to share with me anymore and had gotten Dad to move her bed and wardrobe whilst I was out.

If I'd known Carol didn't want to share anymore I would have happily gone back to my little pink bedroom and I had no intention of having the back bedroom by myself. I pleaded with her to let me have my room back but she would not budge. Then I appealed to Dad to switch the rooms back. He was hardly responsive and coldly repeated that he had no intention of moving any more beds. I felt I had been tricked but no one was listening to my complaint. Surely Mum would see the injustice but she only said she had more important issues to worry about as she potted about in the kitchen.

Later that evening the tension between my sister and I became more intense. I felt this weird mixture of disappointment and anger brewing inside of me as we sat downstairs in the living room. Carol's arrogant air of confidence twisted my stomach. It was obvious that Dad was on her side and he had that cold glare in his eye that was clearly directed at me.

'But it's my bedroom!' I attempted to reason with them. 'I don't wanna be in the back room by meself! - I never said you could have me room!'

'Oh well I ent moving, it ent your room no more it's mine.' Carol insisted.

I looked at Dad. He was stone-faced. No sign of any feelings of sympathy whatsoever. I felt a wave of violence brewing in my stomach. After another attempt at reasoning with the two of them I snapped and lost my temper. Smacking Carol around the head it was the first slap and the only one that landed on target. She was almost twice my strength and her punches came back thick and fast until I was on the floor struggling to get back on my feet.

Dad's voice bellowed over loud and proud, 'Hammer her into the ground' he shouted. And she did.

I struggled to my feet and automatically ran upstairs to my little bedroom but on seeing Carol's belongings there I retreated to the back room. There I screamed and buried my head in the pillow to muffle the sound. Mum came to calm me and reasoned that we would soon enough change the bedrooms back. I felt ever so slightly reassured.

As the days passed it transpired that one of Carol's friends who'd seen my little pink bedroom had commented on how much she liked it and thought it bright, sunny and pretty. Since then Carol had hatched a plan to take it from me and with a genius stroke her mission was accomplished. I was not sure if Dad had been her accomplice or had just been easily manipulated but I suspected the former. Either way he'd condoned it.

I was frustrated and felt betrayed. The back room was dark and damp and hardly received a ray of sunlight. There was nothing spectacular about the view, just an ordinary un-kept back garden and a boring row of houses looking down on me. An old apple tree that was so close to the window that it sometimes tapped on the glass and woke me up in the still of the night. The black shadows of the branches scared me in the dark, waving about as if they were trying to warn me that something bad was about to happen.

I consoled myself with the size of the back bedroom. If I pushed my single bed up in to a corner the area was large enough a space for me to dance in and I could pretend it was a ballet studio. If I ever had the opportunity to take back my old bedroom I certainly would. But that day never came. It was several months before I totally gave up. The front bedroom now had Carol's mark on it and I begrudgingly accepted the back bedroom as my own.

CHAPTER 4

Progressive

It turned out my father had an eye for the ladies and they had trouble keeping their hands off
of him. By the middle of the nineteen-seventies
he had worked his way up in Worcester general
post office to General Manager and continued to
play the trumpet in the dance-bands on weekends.
Both of these positions gave him ample opportunities to have affairs with women and on occasion
he apparently took them. My mother was often
distraught and suffered chronic depression but
Carol and I were oblivious to it most of the time.
Her reluctance to get out of bed became normal
and we had no concept of how she was sometimes
suffering. Mum was often bedbound all day and
there were periods when the house was very un-
tidy and the washing up would be piled high in
the kitchen sink. Wrapped up in our own childish
worlds we didn't take too much notice.

How they had gotten to this point in time - My
father was an only child who originally came from

the city of Leicester and as a young man was 'called up' to national service and joined the Royal Air force. He chose to stay on longer than the obligatory two years' service and in 1960 at the age of twenty three he was 'posted' to the barracks near a small village called Ambrosden in rural Oxfordshire. Soon after his arrival there he left the RAF and got a job locally as a postman. It became his responsibility to deliver letters to the local villagers.

My mother was a naive, innocent and impressionable eighteen year old living in the village of Ambrosden. As a dairy farmer's daughter, she lived in a little thatched cottage with her parents and two older brothers. Destined for a quiet life of Sunday services and baking, she was unofficially betrothed to another local farmer's son. But she became easily infatuated by the young and handsome postman. Used to seeing horses, tractors and other farm vehicles only, she was in awe of this attractive man who sped through the village in his shiny black motor-car on his days off. Soon he was picking her up and taking her out dancing. Seduced by his charm, within a few dates she went from virgin to pregnant. Horrified and dismayed, her parents and older brothers hastily prepared a shotgun wedding in the village church. They crossed their fingers and hoped for the best for her future with this charming unknown entity.

My older sister, Carol, was the product of my parent's early passionate relationship, born in 1961. By that time my parents were married and living in my father's home town of Leicester where my father continued to work in 'Civvy street' as a postman. More than three years passed and I was born in late 1964. Within a few months of my birth, the family moved to the house near the top of the highest hill in the City of Worcester and my father worked in the offices of Worcester general post office with the intention of working his way up the corporate ladder.

By the middle of the nineteen seventies I had fully recovered from pneumonia and learned how to avoid my father and sister at home as much as possible. I loved my ballet lessons and enjoyed playing out on the street with my friends that I'd known all of my life and I loved my animals. Life was not so much idyllic but pleasant enough.

Mum had even improved the back bedroom for me by suggesting we change the old carpet and curtains and I could choose the new colours myself. I picked a purple carpet with pink and white lines staggered through it and shiny white curtains with huge purple and pink flowers. I was thrilled with the outcome. Carol was allowed to have her new carpet and curtains too, as Mum said it was only fair. That annoyed me a little but I soon got over it. I was happy with my bedroom's new look, it seemed quite luxurious.

Most of my school friends lived near to generations of other family members while our grandparents and cousins didn't live in Worcester at all. My Father was progressive and did the new modern thing of taking his young family away from in-laws and all extended family. We were a self-contained nuclear family of four that apparently didn't need anyone else. Carol and I envied our friends who could run around to their grandparent's houses or have the protection of cousins at school.

We did meet up with our extended family once or twice a year but it always had to be planned and as a result we didn't feel much connection to them. Our neighbours, Lisa's parents and Sarah's parents, felt more like our aunts and uncles as they were in our lives every day. Both Sarah and the Mack's had grandparents in the local area so we kind of shared them and were treated like adopted grandchildren.

Our parents were rather progressive in other ways too. Dad was a fundamental Atheist at a time when Atheism was only just coming into the scene. Mum, although raised as a church-going, God fearing Christian, was now more agnostic due to my father's influence. Therefore we were not christened or raised in any religion as such. I did feel a little different to my school friends and ballet friends. As far as I knew they'd all been christened and mostly considered themselves to be Christian - Church of England.

Lisa's family were also unusual, in the area, as they were catholic. And that's why she didn't go to my school; she and her siblings went to the only catholic school near the city centre. When they first came to our street I hadn't known what a catholic was. I had to ask what the word meant. I had no idea of the meaning of faith, the purpose of God parents, or the importance of extended family.

Lisa had a close relationship with her father and all the kids in the street thought he was great. Her mother was a bit changeable, especially lately, we never knew if we should be friendly to her or keep out of her way. She seemed to have strange moods. Sometimes she would be really lovely, chatty and friendly. Other times she was snappy and angry with us like she wanted us out of her sight.

One time Mum went for a chat with Lisa's mum and out of the blue she slapped my mum around the face and said my mum was not to go around her house with her problems as she had enough problems of her own. Mum didn't retaliate although she was shaken up and upset. Saying nothing she just turned around in a dignified manner and quietly made her way back home. I never knew what Mum had been trying to talk to her about but I guessed she'd needed a friend to confide in.

Our two mothers' relationship was never the same again after that day. They still acknowledged each other and had a little chat if they met out in the street but Mum never went around to Lisa's house again although she was invited. Mum would smile sweetly and say that she 'might pop round later' if she was not too busy but she was always too busy and Lisa and I knew that they were no longer real friends.

CHAPTER 5

Best Friends

One Sunday afternoon when I was eleven, Mum hacked into the roast chicken and was detaching the bird's wishbone at the end of the meal.

'You breaks it and you makes a wish Jen.' Mum was joking by deliberately adding S's onto her words like the Worcester folks' did and she had a big grin on her face. Adding unnecessary S's to verbs was part of what we called 'the Worcester lingo' a part that Mum had not picked up so far. She had naturally acquired some aspects of the dialect and accent but it was nowhere near as strong as most of the people who lived around us.

'Stop taking the mick Mum' I rolled my eyes at her.

She hooked the lucky wishbone on to her forefinger and held it out for me to grab the other end. We pulled it and it broke in my favour meaning all of my wishes were bound to come true. So I closed my eyes and made my wish.

'What did you wish for Jen?' Mum enquired

eagerly.

'I wished they'd find Carol-Ann Cooper.' I said. She was still missing without a trace and I felt confident that my wish would solve the problem.

Mum's face dropped to a more serious expression. 'I don't think she's run off with er boyfriend' she said, 'I think someone's took her. We'll not be seeing her again.'

I was taken aback by Mum's statement. She had a sixth sense and was rarely incorrect on her gut feelings. Still I had spent my wish and it was bound to come true so I concluded Mum must have been wrong on this occasion.

With this thought in mind I went to knock on Lisa's door. Lisa answered and quietly stood back to let me into the small reception area.

'Hi ya Lisa, guess what, air Mum thinks someone's took Carol-Ann Cooper!' I went straight in and sat on the bottom stair directly adjacent to the front door. Lisa hadn't spoken yet and I was just noticing how despondent she looked. She closed the door and then with her back up against the wall she slid down to a sitting position next to me.

'Air Mum and Dad's getting divorced' she blurted out as her eyes filled up. I'd not heard of the word 'divorced' before and I had no idea what it meant. Lisa knew - she was almost two years younger than me but she knew exactly what it meant. It had all been explained to her and she spelled it out to me that her parents were going to stop being married, to become unmarried. I'd never heard of such a terrible thing and I felt sorry for Lisa and her brother and sisters. It was such a tragedy. Worst thing was, her dad was moving out and I considered him to be like an uncle. Lisa didn't want to play that day so I went back home and talked to Mum about it.

Lisa's dad soon moved out but at first he came back regularly to visit. Lisa and her siblings were always ecstatic to see him. He was always kind and friendly to my sister and me if he saw us out on the street and even gave us a few sweets when he bought sweets for his own children. But after a few weeks his visits to Hollymount became fewer and further between until we rarely saw him at all.

It became apparent that the Macks couldn't afford to stay living at their house since their father had left. There was talk of Mrs Mack and the children moving out from Hollymount. Lisa and I carried on playing as usual when we saw the 'For Sale' sign being put up. We felt like we would always be next door to each other and really didn't take too much notice.

When the 'Sold' sign went up we started to discuss it. The family were to move to a smaller house nearer to the city centre on the other side of the cathedral, less than two miles away. That didn't seem so bad. The strikingly beautiful cathedral sat on the bank of the river Severn surrounded by beautiful trees and flowers. Lisa and I had played by the river many times on sunny days and hanged about inside the cathedral on several wet days. If they were only moving nearer to the town centre we would all keep in touch. Of course we would. As they all kept saying,' it wasn't a million miles away.'

Our days of being neighbours were numbered. As the countdown began Lisa and I decided to go for a day out to the cinema. We'd heard that the Disney film of Cinderella was showing on the big screen. We didn't have any money for our tickets but we knew it was possible to sneak in through the exit and with nothing to lose we decided to give it a try.

The big old cinema only showed one film at a time and so we patiently waited at the side of the building not knowing when some paying customers might be on their way out after already watching. After about half an hour our patience paid off when a lady with a young child left via the exit stairs. Noticing us looking pensive and ready, she deliberately held the door ajar for us to sneak in. We hurriedly climbed the steps passing several more customers who were on their way out.

Through a swing door we arrived and found ourselves inside the large dusty old theatre. By this time all the customers from the previous screening had left and the cleaners were in picking up discarded popcorn containers and choc-ice wrappers. We ducked down behind the small wall that was behind the back row of seating and hoped we would not be seen. Luckily the cleaners didn't bother to go to the top and as they left we sat down and waited for the film to begin.

Disney's Cinderella was enchanting and Lisa and I were on the edge of our seats thrilled by every moment of the old animated story. The huge theatre was almost empty and we relished having the place nearly to ourselves. We enjoyed the film so much that we never wanted it to end and so when it did end we hid behind the back wall until the cleaners had come and gone again. By the end of the second viewing we knew the words to most of the songs. No more customers came in for the third time we watched it so we sang out loud and danced on the chairs. We did handstands and splits and ran around with pure joy. Our deep friendship caused us to know each other well. We were like the happiest of sisters. We enjoyed every second of the wonderful old film and our time together. After three times of watching we left the building via the side exit so that none of the staff knew we were ever there.

On the walk back to Hollymount we fantasized about how our fairy-tale lives would turn out like Cinderella's. We dreamed of our lavish weddings to our kind, handsome Princes. I pictured my extravagant ceremony in Worcester Cathedral surrounded by the adoration of hundreds of friends and family. My beautiful ivory-white satin and lace dress dragging its train through the ancient church. Arm in arm with my father we would walk down the aisle standing upright and proud. I could see all the relatives and friends wiping their tears of joy. Carol and Mum the proudest of all, sitting in the front row with huge loving smiles.

The day of the house move came and the Macks were busy packing up the removal's van. Within no time at all we were saying our goodbyes but we didn't need to concern ourselves. We expected we would see them all again within a day or two.

Although we occasionally bumped into one or other of the Macks in the city centre, after they'd left Hollymount, we never played out together again.

CHAPTER 6

Baby

I continued to enjoy my ballet classes on Saturdays and since the Macks had gone from the street I would take my lesson at Fletcher's in the city centre and then hang around in town rather than rushing back to Hollymount. Hoping to bump into Lisa, I entertained myself in the many and varied shops. Dad usually worked on Saturdays as he was now the executive manager of Worcestershire general post office. He had reached the top of the corporate ladder and was now in a position of great responsibility. I would sometimes pop in to the public area of the ground floor of the huge building to visit him. There were at least ten counters, exactly like a bank, with a member of staff on each. Usually my father could be spotted walking up and down behind all of the staff overseeing their work and assisting them with any difficulties or troublesome customers they might have. I would always pick a queue and wait in line behind the other customers. Rather than arrogantly pushing to the front just because my father was the boss.

On one occasion I picked a queue and waited patiently behind several customers on a particularly busy Saturday. Dad hadn't noticed me in the crowd on the other side of the counter and was busying himself and looking important in a finely tailored suit as usual. The young lady clerk, who was working at the desk I was waiting at, called him over for some assistance and he came to her and leaned over her shoulder in an inappropriately intimate way that was all too acceptable in those days. The young lady seemed unfazed by this behaviour and Dad must have sorted out her query as within a couple of minutes he'd left her side. Next he was attending to a male clerk's issues, although he did not lean in so closely to him.

A few minutes later and I'd managed to make my way to the front of the queue where I politely asked the lady clerk if I could speak to my dad. When she realised I was her boss's daughter she became very animated and extremely smiley as she attracted my father's attention and pointed me out. Then some of the other clerks that already knew and recognised me were smiling and acknowledging me and saying hello. My father spent a couple of minutes chatting with me as was usual if he could afford the time and I felt really proud of him and proud to be the boss's daughter. Dad seemed quite pleased to see me under these circumstances. Short and sweet perhaps suited him.

Saturday's were still quite fun but Sundays were something else. Since Lisa had left the street, I was often at a loose-end on Sundays. So I generally stayed in my bedroom practising ballet a lot more. Sunday was the only day of the week when the four of us were all at home together. I dreaded sitting at the dinner table as my father would glare at me when I refused to eat something, like he detested me and even in front of my mother the criticizing would begin. He would continue by commenting on how wonderful my sister was and how good that she ate everything and anything on her plate. This was Carol's cue to join in with the barrage of abuse being hurled across the small kitchen table. She would suck up to him in a fake way insisting she was Daddy's favourite -'Daddy's girl' and he would confirm it with his smiles and positive attention towards her.

Mum would be pottering about in the kitchen trying not to add fuel to the fire by getting involved. But on one occasion she did defend me saying I was the straight one and how he just couldn't see Carol's obviously fake behaviour towards him. I genuinely think he didn't care that Carol was acting. He enjoyed it and found her funny, entertaining and endearing because of her sucking up to him. I didn't have the skill required to play along as Carol did. She seemed to understand him;

it looked like she had broken the code and found the key to his heart. I was left on the outside especially when she was around and I felt afraid of them when they teamed up together. Stifled by the two of them I always lost my appetite until in the end the appetite was non-existent in anticipation of the start of a meal.

But these days there was a situation worse than this dreaded mealtime saga. Mum had become very agitated lately. She would snap at us and slam and bang things apparently for no reason whatsoever and overreact to the slightest altercation. I hated Sundays and couldn't wait for the weekend to be over. The bad moods became a regular Sunday occurrence. I thought Mum just didn't like us all being home together but later I understood what was really going on.

It was spring of 1976, I was still eleven and Carol was coming up to fifteen. Every Saturday morning before ballet, my sister and I would wake up and go into our parent's bedroom. Normally both parents would be there so early in the morning but on this day, we found only our mum and there was a note in an envelope left on the bedside table. Dad had left this letter for Mum to inform her that he'd gone to his mother's house in Leicester to 'have a think.' And this is what we discovered on that day - My father had had many affairs and my mother had either forgiven him or tried not to think about it. But something was apparently different this time. The relationship was with a much younger woman at my father's main job at the post office. What a cliché - male manager in affair with younger, female, office assistant.

The radio played,

'You to me are everything, the sweetest song that I can sing oh baby, oh baby'

'To you I guess I'm just a clown that picks you up each time you're down oh baby, oh baby'

Mum couldn't stop herself from shaking. I'd never seen someone fall down from devastation before. Her whole world was wrapped up in our family and it was falling apart. My father was obviously distressed too, although there was little outward sign of it. He really didn't know what to do so he spent a few days at his mother's house in Leicester and then he came back to Worcester and moved in with his girlfriend. A few weeks later he came back to live with us and then months must have passed.

One day, during my last month of primary school, I came home as was usual for my lunch-break and noticed a pram parked inside the gates at the bottom of our driveway. I wondered excitedly, who had come to visit us! I ran up to the steep steps to our front porch door, which was unlocked as usual, and there inside sat a woman who initially I didn't recognise at all. She held in her arms a tiny, new-born baby. I was taken aback at the sight of the tiny child and surprised to see them huddled up and sitting on the floor of the small porch. Happily I smiled and said hello. But this woman didn't smile, she only glared at me.

A wave of confusion and terror washed through me. I rushed past them and into the house through the main door calling out for Mum or Dad but neither parent was home. Only Sandy came running and jumping at me, excitedly wagging her tail as she anticipated a walk. Perplexed, I racked my brains. Who was this woman with babe in arms? On second thoughts she seemed familiar but I just couldn't place her. Maybe this lady was one of Mum's friends or a relative. But why did she look at me with hate in her eyes. I had no idea. I had never known an adult to stare at me in a nasty way like that before and I felt vulnerable being home alone where she could freely follow me in. As an eleven year old child, I was panic-stricken!

Maybe this unknown person had refrained from entering the unlocked door before my arrival because there was a crazy, barking dog inside the house. This may have been the reason she still remained seated in the porch but I wasn't planning on finding out if she was about to come in after me. I gave Sandy a quick cuddle and I went straight out of the back door and down the drive, thus avoiding the woman.

I ran breathlessly to the shopkeeper opposite at Box's shop. Mrs Box had already noticed the pram at the bottom of our driveway. She kindly closed the shop up and took me out into her back garden with some bread and cheese for my lunch. We sat down at a garden bench and this is where Mrs Box explained to me that the woman with the baby was my dad's girlfriend and the baby girl was my dad's daughter! How she knew this detail I didn't know. Maybe Mum had confided in her as a neighbour and friend. I found the idea of the baby being Dad's daughter very farfetched and perhaps in denial I didn't believe it could possibly be true. Mrs Box must have been confused or somehow mistaken.

I spent the afternoon at school with a permanent frown on my forehead as I tried to process the situation. I retrieved the nasty faced image of the woman in the porch and matched it with the animated smile of the office clerk lady I'd seen when I'd joined her queue at the post office. The two images kept flashing through my mind, nasty glare and pleasant smile but I wasn't sure if it could possibly be the same person.

In turmoil I returned home to see the pram still parked in our driveway and this time I was too fearful to enter my home. So I doubled back and ran to the bus stop and waited in the hope that Mum might be on the bus coming back from town. Carol would not be home for some time yet as her senior school was on the other side of the city. As Dad was nowhere to be seen I knew Mum was my only hope.

Luckily Mum was on the bus and pleased although surprised to see me waiting at the stop for her. On the short walk home together I rapidly repeated in verbatim what Mrs Box had said - that Dad's girlfriend and baby were at our house. To my horror, Mum admitted it was true. She said the lady's name was Lois, she worked with Dad at the post office and was a twenty-nine-year-old married woman with no other children. Adrenalin was racing through my body with the fear of what could happen next with this scary unknown female but Mum, perhaps for my sake, appeared very calm.

The pram was still at the bottom of our driveway in full view of all our neighbours. I held Mum's hand as we entered the front porch but now it was empty. There appeared to be no one inside the house either but I could sense someone's presence and my heart was racing. Sandy was behaving strangely, whining and sniffing at the back kitchen door. Since it was a wooden door with three vertical panes of opaque glass inserted, we couldn't see through it clearly. Just shapes and shadows that couldn't be made out with any clarity. The glare of the happy spring sun sarcastically streamed back at us through the door into our bright yellow kitchen. Mum instinctively knew someone was out there and she opened the back door and there they were, the woman and child, lying down in the sun at the top of our driveway. By this time they'd been on our property for several hours. And there was a confusing sight for me. The woman was sunbathing topless and the hungry child was suckling at its mother's breast.

Mum calmly invited the lady in, saying she better get the baby out of the strong sunlight. We sat in the living room together and the woman's demeanour had now changed remarkably since Mum had brought her in and was making tea. Towards me she seemed a lot friendlier and was smiling and chatting instead of glaring. I sat on the carpeted living room floor at the foot of this stranger who was relaxing on our settee now. In my innocence, I was keen and fascinated about the baby and really forgot all about what Mrs Box had told me.

Dad should have been back by now but it was obvious he wasn't coming in to face the music. He'd likely been in the vicinity and noticed the pram in the driveway. He must have immediately scarpered, leaving his wife and daughter to deal with the fall out of his misdemeanours.

The intention of this woman was to take our dad from us firstly by love and sex and then by pregnancy and the birth of his child. When this had still not worked entirely, she'd come to our home with the child to force the issue and it was now getting close to 'mission accomplished.' Mum appeared calm but inside she literally started dying.

That afternoon the woman and baby left and that evening as I tried to sleep I could hear shouting and arguing coming from downstairs. I got up and went to Carol who was quivering and cowering in her bed. We both went to the top of the landing and called down to our parents. Dad came to the bottom of the stairs and reassured us that everything was alright and convinced us to go back to sleep. Mum's piercing screaming escalated but we dared not go downstairs and covering our ears with pillows we eventually must have slept.

Next morning there was a deafening silence and a dark cloud hovered in our once bright and sunny kitchen. Mum had a forced smile on her pale face as she sat alone at the table. I immediately noticed that her right hand was all bandaged up. The kitchen was darker than usual as the backdoor's glass panels, which normally let in daylight, had been crudely covered with hardboard. Mum seemed resigned to the fact that she would need to give us some kind of explanation. She candidly told us how she'd lost her temper and put her fist repeatedly through the three panes of glass, seriously injuring herself in the process. God knows what horrors had taken place that night and the subsequent clean-up we had eventually slept through. We were stunned into preparing our own toast for breakfast before going off to our respective schools in a daze.

Soon after that day, Dad left home for good and

Mum was prescribed something to calm her down by our family doctor. Clinically depressed, she took to her bed in a drug induced stupor only appearing on occasion to walk to the telephone box to converse with her brothers. With a great deal of encouragement from them and the numbing power of tranquillizers, she eventually managed to find the strength to commence divorce proceedings. My two uncles never spoke to my father again

CHAPTER 7

Girls School

The 'six weeks holiday' came and went and then it was time for me to change schools and go to secondary school. This was unfortunate timing as I could have done with less change at this time, not more. My sister had been lucky enough a few years earlier to have gotten into an excellent girls' school and not our local comprehensive that had very poor results. As I had a sibling at the girls' school I was automatically given a place there too. But out of my school year I was the only one who got a place there.

My Victorian style primary school, that I'd attended all my life, was at the end of my street. We could even hear the school bell ring from inside our house. But the girls' school was far from home, two buses away, one to the city centre and then another one out to the other side of town. In contrast to my primary school the uniform was very strict and I had a big bag to carry. I'd never been given a tour of the school and there was no such thing as 'taster days' before the start of the school year. It was a huge, modern style building in comparison to my primary, an institution that I was completely and literally lost in.

My Mother's plan was that my big sister, who'd been attending this school for four years already, would take care of me but Carol clearly didn't want this responsibility. She was in her last year of school and didn't need a little sister cramping her style. She would begrudgingly leave the house with me in the morning and by the time we were around the first corner she would disappear from my sight. Breathlessly I would catch her up at the first bus stop. I soon got used to being ignored on the downhill bus into the city centre. It was a short walk in town to the bus station to locate the second bus. I needed to be highly alert to make sure I didn't lose Carol, in the crowd, as she had no intention of keeping her eye on me.

At the end of the school day we would meet at the gates to supposedly get the two busses back home together but Carol would suggest we walk home and spend the bus fare on sweets instead. I was enticed by the sweets and I kind of had no choice on the decision making as I wasn't capable of negotiating the buses alone. I didn't even know where the right bus stop was and so I would eat the sweets and start the long walk back home.

There was a wedge between myself and Carol, probably caused by the split in the family as my father seemed to prefer her and my mother empathised with me. This wedge caused an extreme case of sibling rivalry that afforded me no help, guidance or assistance from my sister. She was now a strong fifteen year old and I was a weak eleven year old. She didn't want to be seen with me and had no compassion at all.

I knew that feeling of being despised as I'd already had years of it from my father. It wasn't surprising that my sister had been conditioned by him to hate me too. Now I was damn sure she despised me.

My bag was heavily loaded as I carried textbooks, notebooks and physical education kit for every possible lesson of the week. I took everything, every day, because I was afraid of forgetting something and getting into trouble with the teachers. I didn't know how to organise myself and Mum was too depressed to help much. Carol wouldn't help me to carry the bag. She refused to even walk next to me and just raced on ahead until she was a dot in the distance. The walk home would take at least an hour, from the other side of town, through the city centre and then up hill to reach home. I grew more and more exhausted.

Within a few days at my new school I became sick with tiredness and sadness. Completely lost and disoriented I started to weep in lessons and soon I was crying at home repeatedly too. I was constantly faint and dizzy from my lack of sustenance but I couldn't eat. I didn't know what was wrong with me. I would just have an overwhelming feeling of doom come over me from the moment my eyes opened in the morning. In classes my hands would start to shake and I could not control them. I would watch my hands shaking in terror; unsure which had come first, the terror or the tremor. I would be aware of it and then all the other children, children that were strangers to me, would start to notice too. Teachers would just ignore this in the assumption that it would pass.

This was a difficult time for my mum as she was now deeply involved with divorcing my dad and she was not coping well. We had no extended family in Worcester and so the only real support Mum had was conversation on the phone with her brothers. To converse with them she would need to walk to the telephone box. She was a very likeable person, kind and caring. She did have a few good female friends but she felt that as she'd become single, many of them were less keen to associate with her. Perhaps they were afraid she might steal their husbands. This was the nineteen seventies and divorce was still a bit taboo.

After a couple of weeks at the new school my mum took me to see our family doctor who promptly prescribed something to calm me down. This medication would apparently take several weeks to fully get into my system though. So now my mum and I both had the same panacea - Valium.

During this time Mum made a new friend called Iris. An attractive woman that dressed in an immaculate manner and always had a face overly caked in makeup. Her style was very opposite to Mum who had a natural beauty. Iris was obviously richer than us. She drove her own car and her husband apparently drove a Jaguar. I didn't even know what a Jaguar was!

There was something about Iris that I didn't like. Firstly she smoked like a chimney and had no consideration for others who might be prone to chest infection. Secondly she was a bit of a bragger and a show off. Really she was opposite to Mum in every way.

I was clearly suffering from a nervous condition when Iris came to visit. She was starting to become a regular at our house and as on previous visits she was busy chain-smoking in our living room. I entered the room and blinked several times to try to see through the clouds of smoke that were forming.

Iris looked straight at me. 'What's wrong with you?' She said.

'Oh sorry it's just a bit smoky in ere' I tried to be polite and friendly.

'No I don't mean that' She continued, 'ya mum said you're crying all the time!'

'Oh I da' know I just don't feel well' I tried to avoid

eye contact by looking down at my feet. I really didn't want to talk about it and I started to feel myself shake. A lump was forming in my throat and I instantly felt like I couldn't control it.

'Why you crying all the time you know you're too young to have depression don't ya - kids don't get it - you're not old enough so stop being like that you're upsetting ya mum and she's got enough to worry about.' Iris finally stopped to take a drag on her cigarette.

Not sure if I was supposed to reply, I simply said, 'ok' and left the room. Nausea overcame me and I took to my bed. I was dreading the next day of school.

Carol still did nothing to help me settle at the girls school. More than that, she was actively mean to me. She disliked me being there and if she bumped into me her disdain shone through. She did have her own issues after all. Her parents were my parents and we'd both been through a lot. Perhaps her expression of contempt towards me somehow got her through these difficult days.

Anyhow my symptoms got worse and worse. Eventually after a month or so my mother removed me from the excellent girls school on the other side of town and enrolled me at the local mixed comprehensive that had poor results. Ironically, on my last day at the girls school I started to make a new friend and settle a little. But as Mum had gone to so much trouble to get me into the local comprehensive, I never told her that I'd felt a little hope on that last day. I assumed all the paper work was complete, which may well have been the case anyway, and I quietly left.

CHAPTER 8

Forever Severn

Having a September birthday, I was twelve years old by this time and I remember my first day at the mixed comprehensive school, clearly. Mum and I sat in the headmaster's office in the school locally known as Sammie's. He seemed pleasant enough as he put a list in front of me and asked me to point to the class, out of six classes, that I recognised the names of the most children in. There were plenty of names of children from my primary school on this list. The head teacher had asked me which class did I know the most children in - not who was my friend or who did I like the most or who did I consider myself to be as clever as. So I answered the question and the class which I knew the most names in was class number four. So this was the class I was placed in. I didn't realise it at that moment but this was a comprehensive school and the children had been tested and streamed by ability, prior to my late arrival. Sarah, my neighbour and original friend from primary school had gone into class number one, the top set. This is where I would have gone had I been tested but the class I knew the most names in was the fourth set out of six sets and this is where I was placed. The head teacher knew I was taking medication for anxiety/depression and his main priority was to get me settled in. This took precedence over academics.

I hated my first day at Sammie's but after a couple of weeks of being surrounded by faces I recognised, I started to settle. I started to eat a little more and perhaps, by this time, the antidepressants were doing their job.

I settled into my new school relatively quickly. It was an old Victorian building in an area that I knew and more similar in architecture to my primary school. I knew a lot of children from primary school there and soon made new friends too. The school was even close enough to home that I could just about get back during the lunch-break and take Sandy for a quick walk around the block.

I was automatically top of the fourth set in all subjects. But I never moved up to top set. Perhaps it was because the staff knew of my previous mental state and didn't want to rock the boat by moving me up. Or perhaps it was just because it was a poor school in the seventies. I never knew why, I just never moved up and after a while I didn't bother trying.

Instead I threw myself into anything that I thought could improve my chances of becoming a professional ballet dancer! My dance teacher, Barbara, entered me into a ballet show and Mum managed to make me a beautiful white ballet dress for it. It was fitted at the top and made from pure white satin-like material to the waist. The bottom half was layered with slippery white netting and it zipped up at the back. It was beautiful and I couldn't stop trying it on and looking at myself in the mirror. I looked as pure as the white swans that floated along the river Severn. I would wash my hands before even touching the dress and wouldn't let anyone else touch it. It was perfect and I wanted to keep it forever that way.

Although my parents had split up and money was tight, I was lucky that I was still allowed to attend one ballet class per week. But I'd need much more physical activity than that if I were to achieve my dreams of becoming a professional ballerina. Therefore physical education at school became very important as I needed to be very fit to be a dancer. As swimming club was much cheaper than dance class, Mum let me join that too. Training was three evenings a week which would really help me with stamina and overall physical fitness for ballet.

When Dad had moved out from our house he'd taken his records with him including Swan Lake. But that didn't matter; I had the whole concerto recorded in my mind. I knew every piece of music, and every note from each instrument in the orchestra. I could recall it all in my head.

My days of physical weakness and mental fatigue were behind me. I was steadily weaned off of the Valium medication to avoid any relapse and I was managing perfectly well without it. I was popular and sporty and was even elected sports captain of my year. But I only had one dream and I stretched every day for the ballet.

During this time my parents were in the long process of divorcing. As Mum had initiated the proceedings on the grounds of my father's adultery it was her job to prove to the court that he was committing it. Therefore, she was obliged to employ a private detective who followed Dad, his girlfriend and their child, for several months until enough evidence had been collected.

My sister decided she didn't want anything to do with Dad because he'd broken Mum's heart. While I felt confused, on the one hand, he'd broken Mum's heart and I should be loyal to her like my sister intended. But the thought of refusing him made me feeling terribly guilty and tearful. And so I agreed to the weekly meetings alone with him.

Perhaps not so ironically, these next few years included the best moments our relationship ever had. At first my father and I met up regularly on Saturday afternoons. Punctuality being one of his strong points, he would always be dead on time for our regular weekly meetings. For the first few months we went on trips to other nearby towns in the West Midlands. Mum would prepare some cheese and cucumber sandwiches for me to take and she always made double so that Dad could have some too.

After several months we switched from day trips and instead we would go out in the evening to a local sports and social club called Archdale's. This was one of the working men's clubs where my father had played the trumpet at in the past. Dad was never mean to me now and I enjoyed this precious time we spent out together. I got to know more and more people at the club and often Dad would chat with other adults at the bar and I would be off messing about with the other children I knew there.

My very first kiss was in the grounds of the club with a sweet and nerdy boy called Julian. He was a year or two older than me. We used to hold hands and talk and then one evening the kiss just happened out of the blue and was over as quickly as it started. We were both shocked and embarrassed after that. Our immaturity caused awkwardness and we hardly spoke again.

If I fancied a fizzy drink or a packet of crisps I would come back to my dad and he would buy them for me as often and whenever I wanted. During these times my father encouraged me a great deal with my dance studies. He even took me to see the ballet several times at the little theatre in Malvern. I was mesmerised by the dancers and Dad watched the orchestra and happily listened to the classical music. An appreciation of culture and the arts was something we had in common.

As I turned thirteen I joined the school junior brass-band. During my first few weeks as a member, I would carry my cornet to Dad's new house and he would get out his trumpet. We'd stand up straight together in front of his music-stand and he'd give me instruction and advice on how to play.

One day the male music teacher overheard me practising just before the official start of band practise and he whizzed off and came back with the female music teacher. He insisted I repeat some scales and a couple of simple tunes, which I did. The two teachers looked at each-other in bemusement and I was immediately promoted to the senior brass-band.

I became very busy. I was sports captain which in-volved a lot of extracurricular activity. I took bal-let class and practised every spare minute avail-able. I attended swimming club three evenings a week to build up stamina for ballet. I went to Archdale's club on Saturday nights. And now I was a member of the senior school band which had band practise twice a week with a performance during Friday's 'whole school' assembly. I enjoyed school and I enjoyed being busy with all of my activities. I was no longer shy nor seriously underweight.

Sarah had joined the junior brass band a few months before me and shortly after me she was prematurely promoted to the senior band as well. We were both cornet players. Second cornets initially but both of us quickly progressed on to 'first cornets' with the intention of one of us making it to being the band's 'first soloist' one day. That was the top position and the competition was rife between us.

Sarah and I were never close but due to us both being members of the school band we often talked. She sometimes visited me at my house and, as Lisa had gone from Hollymount, I didn't refuse her company. One Saturday afternoon we were talking while I was waiting for Dad to pick me up for his weekly access. I was ready and waiting at the gate as he pulled up in the car. I said goodbye to Sarah but then Dad suggested she should come to Archdale's too if she wanted. I thought this was a fine idea and Sarah quickly ran to check with her mother for permission and then the three of us went out to the club together. Dad was happy to buy us as many fizzy drinks and crisps as we wanted and Sarah and I had a great time.

The following Saturday Sarah came to see me again in the afternoon a short while before Dad was due to come and again Dad naturally invited her to join us. The first time I hadn't minded but now I was starting to be bothered and frustrated. I wasn't sure why. I didn't blame Dad for inviting her; I guess he thought he was just being kind and helpful by not separating us on his arrival.

Every Saturday from then on, Sarah would come to my house 'for a chat' and when my dad arrived he would automatically invite her or just assume she was coming to the club with us. I felt powerless to stop it. I usually had no contact with him from one week to the next and even if I did I didn't know how to ask him not to invite her in advance. Then, when the three of us were together I couldn't say anything and from the time when she came, for a chat before his arrival, I felt too mean to say I didn't want her to come with us or even assume that she intended to come. I always hoped that she would not come for some reason but she always did. I felt robbed of this special time, the only moments I had to be with my dad. Sarah had her own happy family which included her own dad. I was sure her mother was reminding her to run along to us on a Saturday if she forgot. I thought it very selfish to take my dad's time from me but I said nothing and thought myself unkind to think of it.

Dad had set up home with his new girlfriend and their daughter who was now a toddler. Their two bedroomed, terrace house was nicely furnished and his girlfriend didn't seem so bad after all and I became attached to my little half-sister who they'd named Penny. Sometimes they would ask me to baby-sit during my school holidays as they both might go to work in the post office and sometimes on an evening I would baby-sit for them to enjoy a night out. I was happy to have responsibility for my half-sister. They never gave me any money for baby-sitting and I never expected any, after all this was family. Lois asked me to find out about ballet lessons for Penny, when would she be old enough to attend etcetera. So I asked my ballet teacher and soon enough I'd be taking my half-sister along to skip about in primary ballet classes.

Our house was different now. We didn't really go on proper holidays anymore and Christmas became minimalistic. We'd been used to being spoilt with material stuff at Christmas and the difference was now quite extreme. But we were alright and as we knew Mum was doing her best we tried not to complain. She got a job for the first time in her life at Littlewoods food hall; she was usually on the cheese counter.

Even though Dad had let us keep the house and he did pay regular child maintenance and an allowance for my mother's keep, money was still much tighter than when he'd lived at home with us. One example of this is when our green, leather-look three piece suite fell apart. It had been a wedding present for my parents and now was so worn out that the settee had collapsed on one side and so Mum had decided to get rid of the whole suite. I think it was my idea to try to make chairs out of milk-crates. So one day when the shop across the road was closed, Carol and I snuck over and took three, blue milk-crates from outside. I covered them, nicely with table cloths and et Voila, a new three-piece suit was created. It turns out milk-crates are really uncomfortable to sit on and generally I sat on the floor.

We stayed without a settee to sit on which was not great at all but my main concern, as a new teenager, was the embarrassment I felt when friends came in and saw the milk-crates. I hated the thought of people feeling sorry for us. I rarely mentioned the fact that my parents had separated and hoped the majority of my friends didn't know the detail of our circumstance.

Sometimes we complained to Mum. Teenage girls are not the nicest of creatures. We were insular, only thinking of ourselves and how we were not in receipt of the same amount of material objects and holidays. Disappointed and embarrassed that our dad had left and the fact that Mum seemed unable to cope sometimes, we could both become moody and unreasonable on occasion reducing our mum to tears. There was no father, uncle or big brother to keep us in line. Now that I was equal in height and strength to Carol we got along ok in general. But periodically an altercation would escalate and a huge fight would break out. I no longer had to bow down to her.

Mum became desperate to find a new man in her life and started going out to nightclubs with her friend - Iris. Mum was still young after all. I wasn't happy about her leaving us to go out clubbing and would refuse to go to bed until she was home. But sometimes she was so late that I couldn't keep my eyes open and so I would give up and retire to bed.

After a few weekends of going out to nightclubs Mum met her first boyfriend as far as I know. His name was Roy and I instinctively disliked him. More than that, I despised him. He had a distinct body odour that still makes me nauseous when I imagine it now. He smelled like sausages, but not in a good way. I suppose it was just the smell of an alien being in my territory that bothered me so much. And some kind of animal instinct that repelled me and repulsed me.

Since Dad had left home I had taken up residence on his side of my parent's double bed. Until this man called Roy came along. Then I was sent back to my own room. He was much younger than Mum at twenty seven. Mum was now in her mid-thirties and I suppose she had needs but I just didn't know what she saw in him. He obviously fancied my seventeen year old sister anyway and made little effort to disguise the fact, regularly flirting with her openly behind Mum's back though brazenly in front of me. One time I caught him embracing Carol in her bedroom while she was wriggling herself away from his grasp. After a few months Mum's relationship with Roy fizzled out and I was happily back in Mum's bed. But she was out at the nightclubs again still desperate to find someone to replace Dad.

Mum had been taking driving lessons on and off for several years and even before the start of the breakup but now at last she'd passed her driving test and managed to get herself a little second hand car. One day we were on our way to visit Mum's oldest brother, who lived about seventy miles away to the south in Buckinghamshire. Mum was not alright. Stressing about the journey and generally depressed. Carol and I were oblivious to it. We were sitting in the back seat of the car and Sandy (the dog) was at the foot of the front passenger seat. We wanted the dog to come in the back with us but Mum was saying she should stay where she was. But we kept calling out to Sandy as Mum was trying to concentrate on driving and the dog was getting confused as to who she should obey. When Sandy started to clamber over to us Mum got angry and she took her mind off the road for a moment or two. And that was all it took. We smashed into a parked car at the other end of HollyMount. Mum panicked and immediately reversed up and drove off.

Carol and I were stunned into silence and Sandy dropped back down into the foot of the passenger seat. Mum was driving with tears rolling down her face and saying she needed to find Dad to tell her what to do. He was still her security blanket. She drove to the area where Dad now lived with his girlfriend but Mum couldn't work out which house it was and we thought it best to keep quiet. Almost pretending we couldn't remember which house it was either. Eventually Mum thought the better of it and we continued on the journey to visit our uncle and cousins, with the front corner of the car smashed in. Mum was in a terrible state when we arrived.

After much discussion and attempted comforting from her brother, Mum decided to return to Worcester and hand herself in to the police. We went to the police station and Mum explained about the car accident. The owners of the parked car had already reported a hit and run situation. Mum was taken to court and fined heavily for the damage to the other car and especially the fact that she had driven off without initially reporting the incident.

The following Saturday when Sarah and I were at the club with Dad, I told him about the car accident and how Mum had been driving around looking for him in a terrible state of distress.

With a nasty tone, he said, 'What's she looking for me for? I ent nothing to do with her anymore, she shouldn't be out looking for me!' I knew Mum would be hurt by this comment so I never mentioned it to her.

We tried to put it all behind us but Carol and I definitely felt responsible for the accident. It was around this time that I came across Carol sitting alone on our garden swing and she had a kitchen knife in her right hand. She was bending down onto the mud at her feet and cutting worms in half and half again. She was watching them wiggle and seeing how many times she could cut them up before they died. It is only with hindsight that I realise she was disturbed. But at the time I was horrified by this activity and ran in to the house to report to Mum who promptly came outside and reprimanded Carol. Being an animal lover, I was distressed by such an activity. I knew that they were only worms but I couldn't bear to think of any living creature being injured and I certainly couldn't stand by and let it happen.

It reminded me of the time when Lisa's departure from the street was imminent and we were both upset but never discussed our anguish. We'd come across a big black fly that was dying. It had fallen down on the inside window-ledge of my living room. It was just underneath the net curtains and was in amongst its final death-throws. Neither Lisa nor I could consider putting it out of its misery and we wept like babies as we watched it struggling to survive as its final moments slipped away.

As Mum's relationship with the younger guy was

over I felt relieved. However this relief was short lived as within days of the breakup she was going out to night-clubs again. Pushed and encouraged by Iris. I never understood why Iris wanted to go on these nights out. I realised that night-clubs were the places where women needed to go to find a potential husband. But Iris already had a husband so I really had no idea what she was looking for.

Within a couple of weeks Mum became involved with a new man called John. He was just an ordinary guy, neither tall nor good looking but he did have a kind face. There was nothing extraordinary about him other than the fact that he was married and not even estranged from his wife and children. At first I naturally disliked him but he was much nicer than the first boyfriend. He made a big effort to befriend Carol and I but not in a pushy way. Ironically I ended up trusting him even though he was being unfaithful to his wife and therefore the very definition of the word untrustworthy. He seemed to genuinely care for Mum and I didn't have the impression that he fancied Carol, like I did with the first boyfriend. And I suppose time was moving on and perhaps I was becoming more accustomed to my parents being apart.

John worked as a carpenter and I asked him if it was possible to make me a wooden ballet barre to go in my bedroom. I didn't really expect it to happen but one day when I came home from school

Mum told me to have a look in my bedroom. I ran upstairs and was thrilled to see a perfect wooden ballet barre on the floor, waiting to be put up.

Next time John visited he fixed the barre onto my bedroom wall at the exact correct position for my height. Now I could rest my hand on the barre to practise my leg raises and plies'. When I told my ballet teacher she seemed very impressed. Now I was able to practise properly and really push myself at home. Yes I was ecstatic about the ballet barre.

John was unable to visit Mum very often as he had his own family to attend to but I definitely felt more inclined to accept him than I ever did the first boyfriend. At least I had the impression that he was a genuine type of person. Sure he was married to someone else but if Mum could put his wife and children out of her mind then I could do that too. Life was obviously a little more complicated than I'd anticipated.

CHAPTER 9

Cancerous

By the time I was thirteen and a half, my parent's divorce was finally absolute. By now I had passed several grades in classical ballet and my desire to succeed as a dancer was more intense than ever. I dreamed about my move into vocational ballet school. I'd read in a dance magazine that I could audition at fifteen and take up a place in upper school at sixteen. There were several full-time dance schools in England but my first choice, of course, was the Royal Ballet School in London. I could imagine myself there and after a couple of years I would graduate into my career on the stage. I could almost hear the roar of the crowd encouraging me to continue. I'd contracted the ballet at the age of nine and now it was eternally in my blood like a gift, an obsession and a curse.

I was concerned about leaving Mum of course. She'd been on a roller coaster ride lately and not the fun type. Although she didn't smoke and only had the occasional beer, something was wrong with her. She had been feeling unwell and regularly seemed to have pains in her abdominal area. John was at our house one evening when Mum was rolling around on the living room floor, wincing with pain. She was only thirty seven at this time and a healthy weight so at first none of us were overly concerned.

As the days passed Mum's suffering continued and a trip to the doctors rapidly became a hospital stay. Carol and I were home alone while she was in hospital. We understood that Mum was having a full hysterectomy to remove her womb and ovaries. This was going to solve the problem and soon Mum would be well again. A week in hospital was followed by two weeks in a convalescent home by the seaside. This seemed like a long time for Mum to be away from us. We missed her so much. Sarah's Mum, next door, kept an eye on us though and Mum could contact us from time to time via their home phone.

Finally Mum came home and sat down with us at the kitchen table. She looked pale, a tinge yellow and uncomfortable but she was no longer in excruciating agony. She had been told by the doctors that she had had cancer. It was all alright now and the cancer was gone. The doctors had removed it and we could now get on with the recovery.

Cancer - that was a worrying word. I knew that was serious. Carol's eyes filled up with tears and my chin started to quiver. Mum calmed us down.

'I've not got cancer; I've 'had' ovarian cancer! It's been taken away and it's gone now.' She would have to go twenty miles away to Birmingham for something called 'radiotherapy' which would doubly make sure she was cured and all would soon be forgotten. We were slightly reassured and life continued in a normal fashion.

Carol had never been the sharpest tool in the shed and even though she'd attended a good school she'd not achieved much in the way of qualifications. So as she left school she'd gotten a job in a café in the city centre. However this job suited her and she seemed to get on really well with her work colleagues and looked relatively happy. Best thing was, she now had money to spend after paying Mum a little for her keep.

On one occasion, on Carol's day off, I accompanied her into the city centre so that she could go to the many clothes shops. Then she treated me to something to eat. First we went to a café called 'The golden Egg' I had egg, beans and chips and Carol had a burger and chips.

'Where shall we go next?' I said.

Shall we go to the Miramar and get a milkshake?' Carol suggested.

We laughed and joked about and then we went back to the city shops again. We were thrilled to bump into the two older Mack girls in a shop called Chelsea Girl. Of course, I enquired about Lisa but her sisters only said that she was 'not well' and yet there was 'nothing physically wrong with her.' It was all rather ambiguous. So I dropped the subject and instead Carol and I let them quiz us about Hollymount friends and neighbours. They obviously missed their days in our street.

I could not have foreseen that my best friend Lisa was becoming mentally ill. In the not so distant future, and before her teenage years were complete, Lisa would be 'sectioned' under the mental health act and taken by force into an institution. But on that day when I'd met her sisters, I could only see that they didn't want to discuss her and I was blissfully unaware of the severity of the situation.

All in all I had a very enjoyable time out and about with my big sister. When we got on well she could be quite kind and generous.

Carol kept her little bedroom really tidy and her wardrobe was now full of the latest, fashionable new outfits. I was quite jealous as I was now at an age when I was interested in clothes and makeup and I didn't have any fashionable clothes of my own. So, sometimes when Carol was out and I knew she wouldn't be back for a while I would carefully search through her wardrobe for a cardigan or perhaps a blouse that I could borrow for a few hours or so with the intention of her not realising. I would always leave a tiny gap in the wardrobe in the place I'd taken the clothing item from so that I could put it back in the exact same place. I was hoping that I would get away with it but Carol would always realise. She knew instantly her wardrobe had been touched and she would go crazy at me for wearing something of hers and an almighty fight would take place. She would always know exactly what I had worn and I could never understand how she knew when I'd been so careful as to even copy how the buttons had been done up and everything. But Carol was becoming very particular about things being in the right place in general and she was even starting to scrub her hands clean so much, sometimes until they bled.

Mum had another hospital stay after the initial one. She went on to the Birmingham hospital to undergo radiotherapy which made her sick six times a day for six weeks. During this time Carol and I stayed home alone together and Sarah's mum kept an eye on us again. Six weeks was such a long time for us not to see Mum. I missed her and I guess Carol did too. Carol and I got on well for some of the time but it was always a worry for Mum to leave us, on top of all her other worries. I once overheard her telling Sarah's Mum that she was afraid we might kill each other while she was gone. She should never have had to concern herself with such things and we should have been able to control ourselves and have enough maturity to reassure her we would not fight. But we were not so mature.

At the end of the six weeks Mum returned home to us. At five foot and ten inches she was a tall woman and on her return from hospital she weighed six stone. She looked like a walking skeleton and her once thick and vibrant ginger hair was now thin and peppered with grey. But within a few weeks, away from the awful radiotherapy, which may have saved her life, she started to put on some weight and soon appeared to be on the mend.

I was climbing the peak of my own physical fitness at this time. Being petite and strong I was perfect for the ballet. I was slim but muscular and the perfect height and weight to be lifted in a pas de deux. I was full of determination although I worried about Mum. I continued with my hope that I might audition and take a place at a vocational ballet school at sixteen.

But this was the late seventies and there was to be no encouragement for such farfetched ideas. Apparently being a ballet dancer was an impossible dream and one that should be forgotten about. I was encouraged to drop the idea by the school Careers-adviser. Office-practise was apparently a better option for me but I was undeterred. I knew the ballet was going to be a big part of my life. I could visualise a part of myself dancing on the stage to huge audiences.

CHAPTER 10

The George

The nearest public house to Hollymount was called the George. It was a large detached establishment with a lounge and saloon bar but there was also a function room at the rear of the building. Strictly speaking, only over eighteen year olds were allowed in the main bars but not much attention was paid to this rule. Every Thursday night a disco was held in the function room for the over fourteens. This really meant that anyone could attend on disco night and the sight of ten-year olds was not all that unusual. By the age of fourteen I was a regular at the George pub disco. I was friendly with many of the adult punters who sometimes came into the disco as well as children of my own age.

A couple of men in their mid-thirties were also regulars at the George public house. Terry and his friend, who I only ever knew as Butch, were always really friendly to me and would normally buy me fizzy drinks and give me a lot of attention. Sometimes I would go into the function room disco and if they were not there I would go through a connecting door and find them in the Saloon or the Lounge bar. Butch was the better looking of the two. He was tall and big and I guessed that was why he'd acquired his nickname. I'd heard a rumour that he'd been in prison but I never knew or asked why. It was not my business and anyway he'd served his time.

Whenever Butch saw me his eyes would light up and he would put his arms out to me in a gesture to sit on his knee in full view of the other punters who didn't take much notice. I would happily oblige him. These two men would chat and laugh with me for most of the evening and I lapped up their attention. Sometimes I would pop back into the disco to have a dance and talk with friends of my own age. But if I wanted a soft drink or even something stronger I was to come to Terry and Butch and they would always get me whatever I wanted without hesitation.

On one occasion, when I was perched on Butch's knee, an attractive woman in her late-twenties came up behind him and draped her arms around his neck. My blood ran cold and I was agitated inside. Why had this woman blatantly ignored the fact that I was sitting with Butch and who was she and how dare she! Maybe she'd ignored my being there because she thought of me as being like a child on a father's knee, the thought made me angry and my expression must have made it clear I was upset. Butch didn't give her any encouragement and she was gone in a minute or two. Butch and Terry could see I was troubled and they gave each other a knowing smile. Butch gave me a reassuring hug and I was instantly consoled and felt protected and important to him.

These two men were often driving about in a large blue work-van. When I saw them out and about, they would stop, smile and have a little chat with me. I looked forward to seeing them and always kept an eye out for the blue van when I was walking out and about in Worcester.

One evening my mum went for a quiet drink with John at the George and she caught sight of me sitting on Butch's lap in the main saloon. When Butch got up to go to the bar Mum followed him, took him to one side and politely asked him to keep away from me. Later that evening she had a talk with me and tried to explain the reasons why I shouldn't be associating with Butch and Terry. I didn't understand what the problem was and felt upset at the thought of losing these friends. I overheard Mum telling John that I was looking for a 'father figure' and I was confused by the whole thing. All I knew was that I really liked Butch and I couldn't wait to see him again. He was kind to me and very good looking, why wouldn't I like him. Mum probably just didn't like these two because they had tattoos. She was a bit old fashioned in that way.

Then one disco night I was pleased to see Butch and Terry in the function room on my arrival at the George. Naturally I sat with them and as usual they supplied me with drinks. A slow record came on, 'Bridge over troubled water.' Butch pulled me up onto the dance floor and held me close to him. When the music stopped he sat me on his knee and gave me a little kiss. I felt a mixture of embarrassment and excitement. I was totally infatuated by him and I was thrilled by his apparent love and affection.

Next thing Butch was asking me to go outside with him so that he could give me a 'real kiss.' I was in awe of him as he held my hand and led me past the others. As soon as we got to the entrance porch as if he could not wait a second longer Butch pressed me up against the wall and started kissing me with a force that I'd never before experienced. I could only draw upon my experience with Julian, that sweet boy and that soft, organic kiss.

At first, I tried to kiss Butch back but I suddenly felt completely out of my depth. Before I knew it, he'd taken my hand and pressed it up between his legs. I felt a wave of fear but I didn't want to offend him and so I left my hand where he'd placed it but I did not know what I was supposed to do with it. He helped me by moving my hand for me but my body language by now was clearly saying I was not comfortable with this situation.

I started to freeze as new customers were starting to pass by us in the entrance porch. Most of the people that passed didn't pay any attention but one lady caught my eye and I had the feeling she wanted to say something. She could see I was young and Butch was old enough to be my father. The lady hesitated but Butch didn't look like the type you would want to argue with and at this moment he was driven like a guided missile. Nothing was going to stop him easily, he was hyped. The lady looked over her shoulder with a sorry or concerned expression and then walked on into the pub.

Butch was slightly distracted by the disturbance of the passing punters but he was now pressing himself up against me and I was caught between a rock and a hard place. He whispered in my ear that we should leave the porch and go around to the side of the building where it was private and secluded. In his eagerness to have me he'd made a mistake. He'd not been able wait a second longer and he'd commenced in a place where it would be impossible to continue. He needed me to consent to the change of location as if he was too pushy I might cause a fuss. Too many people had already seen us.

By now I felt embarrassed and out of control. I didn't want to go to the secluded spot as I started to realise what might happen there. Butch had his hands all over me and by now I was starting to struggle out from his grasp.

Soon some more people were arriving and passing us in the porch. My body was stiff and I wanted to be back inside in the comfort of the crowd. At this point Butch calmed down a little and suggested we go back in. We returned to the function room and he told me to sit with Terry while he got the drinks in. I felt much better to be back inside and we continued to enjoy each other's company. But I began to realise what Mum had been concerned about. I blamed myself for leading Butch on and I never discussed what happened that night with anyone.

A few days later and I noticed the blue van coming towards me. I stopped and waved but the van did not stop and as it passed only Terry was inside, waving. The following week I went to the George with the intension of chatting with Butch but only on the inside of the building where I felt more in control. I needed to be more careful not to get myself into a position with him again, I was far from ready. My feelings were really confused as I still wanted his attention. I might have loved him but whether it was the love of lovers or that of daughter and father or a mixture of the two, I never knew.

The following week Terry and Butch didn't turn up at the pub. I was disappointed not to see them. Then several weeks passed and Terry started to come to the pub on his own and he would chat with other men so I found it difficult to ask him about Butch. A little more time passed and eventually I heard a rumour that Butch had 'gone away' and that meant he was in prison. No one seemed to know why or if they did know the subject appeared to be too taboo to discuss it with me. I never found out why he'd gone away. With hindsight it may have been for the best. But hindsight is a terrible thing.

CHAPTER 11

Sandy, Fred and Flynn

Although John was married to someone else he seemed to have a deep love and concern for my mum as their relationship continued to blossom over the next year or so. Of course it wasn't always easy for them to spend time together as he had his own wife and children to attend to but it was obvious he loved Mum dearly.

After a brief reprieve from the illness Mum was sick again. Unfit to work and in receipt of invalidity benefits and the supporting evidence of doctors, she took the opportunity and made arrangements for us to move out of our privately own house and into a council flat a couple of miles away. With the money from the sale of our house we would be able to furnish the flat beautifully. So instead of living in a lovely, large three bedroom house with poor worn out furniture and carpets we would live in a small two bedroom flat but we would have brand new, luxurious furniture and carpets. Also, Mum was thinking ahead, if anything did happen to her, this two-bedroom flat would be a suitable home for my sister and I. We would not have to worry about money for a while as there would be some left over from the sale of the house after the new place had been furnished.

Obviously I couldn't take my rabbit to live in a council flat with no garden and luckily a scruffy girl at school called Julie was happy to take Flynn. This girl was bullied at school and one of the rumours going around about her was that she and her family ate the pet rabbits that they kept. I hoped that this was just a vicious lie and never knew if it was true or untrue. Either way Flynn the rabbit had to go and Julie's family was willing to take him. Julie and I managed to carry the rabbit-hutch between us more than a mile to her house. I was a little despondent about losing my rabbit but there wasn't much choice and I convinced myself that Julie would take good care of Flynn.

Just a few weeks before we were due to move house I went on a school adventure holiday to Snowdonia in Wales. The anticipation of it was so exciting. The lists of activities were endless. Including abseiling, rock climbing, rafting etc. Also I would get to spend a week away with my school friends in the beautiful Welsh countryside.

There was an all girl's dormitory with several bunk beds. We were all so excited that we stayed awake all night chatting on the first night which was a big mistake as we needed a lot of energy for the next day's adventure. We were told to wear our usual clothes such as jeans and a jumper and on top of this we were dressed in special, green, heavy clothing that had been used time and time again by previous adventurers. Then on top of the green clothing they covered us in orange water proofs. We were given heavy green worn-out walking socks to go on top of our own socks and then heavy walking boots that had been worn by many before us. Little attention was given to correct sizing and ill-fitting clothes and boots seemed to be expected and accepted. Finally we were kitted out with a heavy green balaclava and an ill-fitting orange hard hat. Now we were really ready for our 'adventure'.

Over the week we were driven in a mini bus, every day strapped up in our adventure outfits. We would be dropped off at different locations over the Welsh hills and then we would walk for miles carrying equipment for our lunch stop. I was one of the fittest girls so I offered to carry the camping stove in my backpack while others carried other equipment and tins of food. Some of the walks were really tough with the Welsh rain pushing us backwards and our feet full of blisters. Some of the girls were crying and pleading to go home or sometimes refusing to continue walking. At one point I carried another girl's rucksack as well as my own while trying to talk to her to encourage her to keep going and distracting her from the effort. It wasn't much fun, I guess they called it 'character building'. Although we were tired we still didn't sleep much in the dormitory and by the last day we were exhausted and certainly wanting to go home.

On the last trip in the mini bus I started to feel really squashed on the back seat. I could hardly move with the amount of protective clothing and I was washed out from the week of 'character building' exercises. Also I was worrying, soon I would be going home and soon after that we would be moving house. I felt really hot and uncomfortable. I couldn't move, I couldn't breathe and my heart began to race, I started to feel dizzy. Then a strange feeling of doom and panic came over me like my best friend had just died. I started to cry and all the girls in the bus called out to the teacher who had a seat next to the driver.

They stopped the mini bus and the teacher pulled me out from the rear of the bus whereby she promptly stripped off my top layers of clothing and then found me a slightly more spacious seat. I managed to calm down and forgot about the squashed feeling and the day continued and the 'adventure holiday' came to an end. All of us girls were happy to be on the coach on the way back to Worcester and when we met up with the boys they were thrilled to be going home too.

Although I had felt awful at the time I soon forgot about the panic I'd experienced. I was glad to be leaving the 'adventure' behind and looking forward to seeing Mum and Carol. I knew that Sandy, my mixed-breed dog, was going to be really overexcited on seeing me and would be expecting a walk straightaway.

When I arrived home, Carol was out and Mum was home with John. I said hello to them and with an animated smile I called out to Sandy. Normally Sandy would be so thrilled to hear me come home that she would come running and nearly knock me over. But on this day there was no sign of my dog. Perhaps she was sleeping upstairs on my bed. I ran up the stairs calling out 'Sandy, Sandy!' This was odd. I checked all the rooms; they were almost packed up ready for our house move. No dog. I came downstairs and looked at Mum and her boyfriend. They both looked terrible, stone white and upset. Mum looked ill and she had a strained look on her face.

Mum began speaking, 'I'm sorry Jen, so sorry, I had to do it - there was no other choice, we couldn't take a dog to live in a council flat - it's against the rules!' I was horrified as she continued, 'We took Sandy to the vet while you were away and she's asleep now.' Tears flowed down her face and John looked as if he was about to burst out crying too.

'You mean she's dead!' I felt a wave of horror hit my heart as I struggled to continue to speak, 'How could you do that? Why didn't you get someone else to av her?'

John opened his mouth and also struggled to speak, 'We tried Jen but no one wanted her.' Sandy was an unpopular type of mixed-breed dog and a little wild. Mum had too many other worries and she'd done what she thought was best at the time. I started to back away from them - devastated.

Mum tried desperately to improve the situation, 'The good news is, with permission its ok for us to have a cat at the flat. We've checked with the council and they've given their permission for Fred to come with us!'

I ran to my empty bedroom. It looked different now. My huge collection of toys and other belongings were all packed up in boxes and ready for our move. My ballet barre had been taken down from the wall and was on the floor. The plan was for it to go up on my new bedroom wall at the flat.

I threw myself onto my bed and called out for Sandy. I could visualise her sad face looking at me, calling out for me to help her. What must she have thought when they took her in the car to the vet. When she felt the needle of death enter her paw. She must have been looking for me like she always did.

'I see a memory'

'I never realised'

'How happy you made me oh Sandy'

'Well you came and you gave without taking'

'But they sent you away oh Sandy'

'And you kissed me and stopped me from shaking'

'And I need you today oh Sandy'

I stayed in my room and wept for hours and I could hear Mum crying downstairs too.

A couple of weeks later we moved out of the Hollymount house, from the place I'd lived all of my life. We took Fred (the cat) for his first ever trip in a car with us and I clung onto him as he struggled to break free.

CHAPTER 12

Protection

There were several blocks of flats in a huge council estate in a rougher part of town. The area was still on our side of town but even further away from the city centre than Hollymount. Ours was the middle flat out of three floors. As we were used to having our own detached house the sounds we got from the surrounding flats were a bit of a culture shock to us at first. The flat directly above us was particularly noisy. I noticed almost immediately that they had ignored the 'no dogs' rule and kept two large dogs!

My fluffy black cat, Fred, was very unhappy. He'd lived at our old house since being a kitten and Mum said cats didn't like being moved. We were worried about letting him out of the flat in case he didn't return. Mum had arranged to have the flat furnished with all new carpets, a new settee and beds. Everything was new. This was good for us but probably very confusing for a cat with all the new smells. So we kept Fred in for a week or two. But he was an outdoor cat and he cried repeatedly at the door to go out. Mum was not well enough to deal with this and one day when I was at school she let him out. Apparently he'd hesitated on the stairwell and looked back almost as if to say 'goodbye.' He didn't return to us.

I searched high and low for that cat. I even went back to Hollymount a couple of miles away but none of our old neighbours had seen him and we never saw him again. Maybe someone else was caring for him now. But I guessed he was either hit by a car or he'd just got tired and laid down and died on his attempt to get back to his old territory. I was so sad. Not knowing what happened to poor Fred stayed with me forever.

I could still walk to school from our new home but it was much further away than from our old house. So I didn't come home for lunch anymore. There was no dog to walk anyway. There was one good thing though - our new home was closer to Archdale's club and I was able to go there any evening by myself. I still went there with my dad on Saturdays too, now without Sarah as she could no longer get herself invited from this position. The best thing of all, on Friday nights it was disco night!

It was at the Disco that I'd spent the night of my fifteenth birthday a few months prior to the house move. It had been a great day. Mum had taken me to the ballet shop in Malvern and bought me a new pair of pointe shoes and a huge hard back book called 'The Colourful World of Ballet' that I really loved and a bottle of expensive perfume. It'd felt like a very special birthday indeed.

Then in the evening I'd gone along to the Friday night disco and there I met a guy called Dave. He wasn't bad looking with his brown eyes, straight brown hair and goofy smile. He told silly jokes and made me laugh. He was nineteen and un-employed. This was not unusual. There was high unemployment in the West Midlands at that time. Dave clearly wanted to make an impression on me and he did.

Over the next few weeks Dave and I met up at Archdale's Friday night disco. Sometimes we'd meet during the week too and held hands whilst walking in the park. I saw a lot of him over about a month. I soon realised he was making a big effort to impress me with talk about fights he'd been in and drugs he'd taken. I didn't know if any of his stories were true and their truth or falsehood was of little consequence to me. What concerned me was that he would think these stories might have a charming effect on me. Either he'd really done the things he'd purported to have done, which put me off of him or he was making it up, which also put me off of him.

I started to regret behaving like Dave's girlfriend as I was going off of him rapidly. The less inter-est I showed him the more besotted he became.

He started to get really clingy and bizarrely began to talk about us getting engaged. Looking back I guess he was pushing for sex and thought the engagement might do the trick. I started to dislike him to the point that he repulsed me. As I planned to break up with him he became verbally aggressive and as he walked me home one day I told him it was over. He pushed me up against a wall and shook me by the arms.

'Don't leave me Jen, don't leave me!' he repeated, until I twisted myself away from him and released his grasp. I thought about Butch, if he knew about this he would most probably sort Dave out! I felt sure that he would have protected me. I'd been only fourteen during my 'relationship' with Butch and now that he was still in prison I had no one. I had no brothers to stand up for me and I felt a bit afraid of Dave's erratic behaviour. So I turned to my father for guidance and assistance but he just refused to get involved.

After that day I managed to convince myself that Dave had accepted my rejection and I started to feel I could put it all behind me. I thought I'd made things clear. But at the following Friday night disco he still wouldn't leave me alone. He followed me around and blatantly insulted me even in front of my girlfriends.

'You'm just a slag' he insisted. Then a few minutes later, 'I wants to talk to you Jen, can we just go outside a minute?' When I shook my head he continued, 'Everyone knows what a slut you are.' I was confused. Why was he talking to me like that? Did people truly think so badly of me?

I went to the bar, choking back on tears, to get away from him and to order a drink. A man called Tommy worked behind the bar. He was a big guy of about my father's age. He had overheard everything and on seeing my distress he came out from behind the bar and marched straight over to confront Dave on my father's behalf.

'Leave her alone you idiot! What's the matter with you? Tommy began, she don't wanna be with you and if I catches you near er again I'll smack your face in!'

There was a moment of hush until Dave replied, 'All right Tom alright, I don't want no trouble.' With that he immediately left the bar area and disappeared into the loud music and the flashing lights of the disco hall.'

Finally, thanks to Tommy's fatherly concern for me, I could relax again at the club. Dave still had his eye on me and I was aware of that but over time I felt sure he would accept the situation as it was and move on to someone else.

Mum was really unwell during that time and I felt that telling her about how Dave had been upsetting me was upsetting her. We spent an evening with Mum lecturing Carol and I about the dangers of getting involved with certain types. We all seemed to be on the same page and in agreement that we needed to be more careful in the future. I'd made an immature error of judgement, Tommy had solved the problem and I had not only learned a valuable lesson but my sister had learned something too it seemed.

A couple of months later and it was New Year's Eve. I'd had no more conversation with Dave although I had seen him in passing many times at the club. Now and then if our eyes met he would give me a nod of the head as acknowledgment that he'd seen me and out of politeness I did the same back with a half-smile. The occasional full smile succeeded until I felt he was over me and I put our short-lived affair out of my mind.

Carol and I spent the evening and the countdown to the start of 1980 at Archdale's club. We heard there was going to be a party to follow at Dave's house where he lived with his mum, dad, brother and little sisters. Carol and several others were considering going along too and since Dave seemed to be over me, I felt tempted. My friends tried to convince me I'd be safe enough with them. I guessed there was safety in numbers and no harm could really come to me at Dave's mum's house. Many of my friends were asking if I was going on to continue the celebration there. It wasn't any ordinary New Year's Eve; we were saying goodbye to the nineteen-seventies. It was the first turn of a decade most of us could remember.

In the end I decided it would be risky to enter into Dave's domain. I thought about all the things Mum had said and how she was home alone. I decided that I had no intention of ever going in to Dave's family house and so I made my way home to be with Mum. As we'd previously discussed the trouble I'd had with him, she was pleased I hadn't been so stupid as to go inside his house. She said it was unfortunate that Carol had gone along to the party. Mum also said that Dave was 'a wrong un'

To make things worse, much worse, Dave had apparently made a beeline for Carol at the party and they'd spent the early hours of 1980 snogging on his staircase. I had a mixture of emotion when Carol had relayed the information with apparent indifference to my feeling on the subject. Confusion, disappointment and dread that Dave was somehow back in my life. I felt sure that he was only trying to make me jealous or be with my sister to be closer to me. My opinion, unsurprisingly infuriated Carol who naturally concluded that I was jealous. I told Carol to stay away from him for her own sake and Mum told her too. We knew he was trouble, but Carol wouldn't listen. She jumped straight into a relationship with him. This turned out to be the biggest mistake of her life.

So in the March of 1980 we moved to the council flat. Dave and Carol were now a couple and she was out most of the time with him. His parent's council house was in the area we'd moved to and he had

a large extended, rough family that all lived locally to us. I kept out of the new couple's way and
often didn't see them as they would stay over at
Dave's aunt's house. So now it was just Mum and I
in the flat.

I continued with my ballet lessons but they were
starting to become a struggle. John hadn't got
around to putting up my ballet barre yet and we
were much further away from the dance studios
now on the wrong side of town. Still I sometimes
managed to cycle to the lessons and chain my bike
up outside.

We'd been living in the flat for a couple of months
and Mum was looking more and more unwell. In
fact she was sick every time she ate. Even drink-
ing water could induce vomiting. She was really
bedridden and I was trying to take care of her but
I couldn't pretend that I was any good at it. I had
no clue how to really do anything. Only pop to the
shop for milk and maybe push the vacuum cleaner
around. I hadn't really learned how to cook or
clean properly yet. Since Dad had left and Mum
was ill I'd become a little feral at a time when I
should have been learning these things and now
Mum and the flat needed taking care of and I didn't
know how. I remember holding her hand and making her bread and butter but she couldn't keep
it down and was losing weight again, drastically.
Even though she was clearly very ill, I still didn't
realise or maybe I refused to accept it.

'Jen' Mum called out with a weak voice.

'Yeah Mum, what is it?'

She was removing her rings from her left hand.

'Can you put these rings in that little white box over there on the side' Mum said. There was no fat left on her bony fingers and the rings fell away easily. 'Now will you look after them for me Jen?'

'Yeah of course I will, I'll put them in me bottom draw' I said as I carefully placed Mum's gold wedding band and opal and sapphire engagement ring into the little white box as requested. 'I don't know why you still wears 'em anyway - I mean now that you'm divorced?'

Mum tried to shuffle into a sitting up position but she hardly had the strength to manage the manoeuvre, so I tried to assist. Then after a few shallow breaths she continued.

'Well you know - I never stopped loving ya dad' she said as she closed her eyes and tears dropped down on both cheeks simultaneously.

'It's ok Mum, don't worry, I'll look after em and when you puts weight back on you can wear em again' I closed the little box and bounced out of the room to place it in my bottom draw.

'Jen' Mum called out again, 'You know - if anything happens to me, your uncle Brian will look after you - don't you?' She was referring to the brother she was particularly close to. He'd reassured her that no matter what, he'd make sure that I was ok.

'Well yeah, I knows that but I don't know why you'm saying it?' I really didn't know.

'Can you pop down to the telephone box and call the hospital, tell them your mum's not well, tell them my name, they need to send an ambulance.' Mum said.

'Alright I will,' I sat on the end of the bed for a few seconds, 'I loves you Mum.' As I said it I realised I didn't say that very often. In fact I couldn't recall ever saying it before.

'I love you too Jen' Mum closed her eyes.

I grabbed a five pence piece off of Mum's bed-side cabinet and my denim jacket from the hook next to the door and I ran to the telephone box. I was thinking, the quicker they get Mum into hospital the sooner they'll fix her up and send her back home.

The hospital sent an ambulance and when it arrived, Mum tried to stand up but her legs were too weak and she wobbled back down onto the bed. One of the paramedics rushed back out to get the stretcher and Mum was carried out on it. I stood on the street and watched the ambulance drive off and then I was home alone.

I watched television for a while and then I got myself to bed and next day I went to school. In the evening Carol came to the flat and was upset to learn that Mum was back in hospital. She was angry with me with me for not keeping her informed. I was angry with her for leaving me alone with Mum. She grabbed a few items and stormed back out. After the argument I started to feel terribly frustrated and distressed. Like a prisoner in solitary confinement I walked around the walls of the flat pacing up and down. In the kitchen cupboard I found a bottle of Cognac, a moving-in present for mum from her friend Iris. Although it tasted awful, I started to pour it down my throat with the hope of numbing my pain. Within half an hour I'd drank the lot and the whole building started to spin around me. The floor was moving as I stumbled out of the flat crying and going in and out of consciousness.

I was found out in the street by Kev the disc Jockey from the Friday night disco. He literally picked me up and carried me to his mother's house who called an ambulance while I was vomiting on their living room carpet. In a drunken stupor I cried out for my mum.

I was taken to the hospital and there I was apparently given a stomach-pump while unconscious and put to bed on a different ward to Mum. She wasn't told that I'd been admitted until the next day when I was well enough to be discharged. Before I left I was introduced to the hospital social worker. He was a young, dark haired man called Derek. He gave me his telephone number. If I ever needed anything I was to call him.

Then I went to Mum's ward. She looked awful, her colour was yellow and she'd just been told about me. On top of everything else she was worried sick about me. I felt so ashamed and I had no idea why I had done what I had done.

CHAPTER 13

Abide with me

It was the summer of 1980 and Mum had been in hospital for a week or two and by now I'd recovered from the alcohol poisoning. I'd been staying in the flat sometimes alone and sometimes Carol would stay there too. I'd been getting myself up in the mornings and off to school every day.

In the warm summer evenings I walked about three miles to the hospital to visit Mum. One evening Dad picked me up in his car and took me to see her. Mum still loved Dad that was evident and perhaps he still had feelings for her too. It was strangely uncomfortable being there together with the both of them again. But Mum's illness was of paramount importance now and nothing else really mattered. The next day she would have another operation to save her life.

I was overwhelmed with emotion when I kissed her and said goodbye. I never really understood my feelings as to why I felt embarrassed to express emotion in front of Dad but I managed to hold back the tears as he was next to me. As I left, I looked through the window and Mum looked back at me. I wanted to run back and throw myself into her arms and cry 'don't leave me Mum - please don't die!' But I did not. I didn't want to be vulnerable in front of Dad. We left and Dad dropped me off at the flat.

Next day I got myself off to school. I was a wreck and started crying in biology class. A class-mate told the teacher that I was upset as I thought my mum was dying. The teacher took me to one side and shook me.

She said, 'Your mother is not going to die! Repeat after me - My mother is not going to die!'

'My mother is not going to die' I repeated in a mechanical fashion.

Then I asked if I could have the afternoons off to go to 'visiting' at the hospital but the teacher said 'no' as I had some academic tests in the afternoons. She shook me again and repeated that my mother was not going to die and that I could see her in the evening visiting sessions.

It was a beautiful summer's evening of June the seventeenth 1980. It was Dad's birthday. Carol had already been to see mum at afternoon visiting at the hospital and reported that she hadn't looked at all well. The operation was complete but the doctors didn't have much in the way of hopeful news. I'd been unauthorised to take the afternoon off school even though I pleaded with my teachers. My mock-exams were very important, more important than visits to mum it seemed. I could easily wait and go to the evening visiting sessions at the hospital they'd said.

My sister was now eighteen and I was fifteen and we were attracting a lot of attention from teenage boys and young men. A couple of boys that we knew stopped us for a chat as we were walking. We had a little laugh and a joke with them, and then we continued on our way to the hospital. It was quite a walk on a hot summer's evening. The coolness of the hospital was a welcome relief.

We entered the hospital and made our way to our mum's ward. But as I went to push open the ward door, Derek (the hospital social worker) pushed the swing door back to come out of the ward. He prevented us from going in to mum's ward and told us to come with him to a little side room. We followed him.

We entered a room with several comfortable chairs but the young man didn't think to ask us to sit down. I suppose he thought only older folks needed a seat when being told shocking news. So I stood next to Carol as Derek stood directly opposite us and these words came out of his mouth, 'I'm afraid your mother has died.' His words echoed in my ears.

Carol immediately started to cry and I felt a rush of emotion and my legs collapsed. Next thing I was on the floor in a heap and Carol was trying to help me to stand up but I couldn't stand. I'd lost all strength in my legs. For several moments we were both on the floor in a fit of tear and a state of utter shock and despair. Then Carol begged, 'Please Jen, please get up!' Eventually she managed to support me to my feet, while Derek stood looking at us as if surprised by our reactions.

Then Derek directed us to a small side room back on the ward where Dad was already sitting. A kind nurse was making tea and trying her best to explain things to us in a tactful manner. She explained that the operation had taken place in the afternoon of the previous day. The doctors had put mum to sleep and opened her up with a vertical incision. She'd already had her womb and ovaries removed horizontally. On seeing her internal organs they'd decided that she was 'riddled with cancer.' All of her organs were covered. They'd decided that 'nothing could be done' and so they 'stitched her back up.' Unable to cope with the trauma of a major operation, that evening, she went in and out of coma. On this afternoon, the seventeenth of June, Carol had visited and Mum was incoherent. As Carol cried her tears fell on Mum's face. She'd hoped for an improvement by the evening. But only a terrible death came.

From the hospital we went to Dad's house and his

girlfriend, Lois, was kind to us. That evening a bed was made up for us on the floor of their daughter's bedroom. Penny went to sleep with them and we went through the motions of trying to sleep. I fell asleep and woke up several times crying, hoping it was just a bad dream. I wanted to howl out like a dog with a broken leg but I knew I shouldn't wake anyone. The pain was truly unbearable.

A few days passed with Carol and I holding back the tears as far as we could. I didn't know if Carol felt the same but I really didn't like crying in front of Dad. He was acting oddly, although kind of normal for him. He kept insisting on playing loud records like the theme tune to the Oliver Twist musical.

'Can you just turn that off?!' I shouted over the music.

'Oh let's all just sit around and be morbid then shall we?' he said.

'Well our mum has just died!' I replied, showing infuriation in my tone.

Carol's exasperated expression showed she agreed with me. 'I'm gonna go and check on the flat' she announced.

'I'll come with ya' I said.

'No, you stay ere with Dad. There's no point in us both going. You'll be better off staying ere. I'll just check everything's ok and I'll be back later on.'

She insisted.

'Well how long's you gonna be?' I didn't want her to go without me.

'I'll only be a couple of hours, I won't be long.' She said.

She clearly wanted to go by herself. I couldn't push it anymore. She wouldn't let me go with her, so I respected her instruction to stay put. Off she went and I waited for her return.

What followed was almost a rerun of the Back-Room chapter.

The hours passed and I started to wonder what Carol was doing at the flat for so long. By bedtime she was still out so I guessed that as it had got dark she'd decided to sleep there and would come back to Dad's in the morning. The next day came and went. I was thinking to go and look for her but I guessed that if I left she would come back and we'd end up missing each other by taking differ-ent routes. Then she would end up back at Dad's and I'd be there. Dad said to wait and she'd be back soon enough. Although Dad had a home telephone Carol didn't call. Well Dad didn't mention any telephone conversation with her. I supposed she thought there was no need to call. By the fourth day of waiting I realised she wasn't coming back. Maybe she was waiting, at the flat, for me to come to her. I decided it was time to leave Dad's house too and I walked the three miles back to the flat.

As soon as I arrived, I knew he'd moved in. Dave. My sister's boyfriend, my ex-boyfriend was living in my flat. While I'd been waiting for Carol to return, she and Dave had been setting up home together. They'd already been to the council and our mum's tenancy agreement had now been passed on to my sister's name. She was eighteen and legally able to have the flat in her own right. Therefore it was now officially her place and Dave was entitled to live there too if she so wanted. Initially I naturally assumed it was still my home and for three days it was.

Until Carol announced, 'Dave doesn't want you ere, you'll have to live with Dad'.

I made a feeble attempt to reason with her but she was adamant that I should go and stay with Dad for now at least. I packed up a few necessities in an orange suitcase and a couple of boxes with the idea that Dad would pick them up for me later. Then I took what I could carry for the time being and left the majority of my belongings in my bedroom at the flat. I got on my bike and cycled back to Dad's house with carrier bags on both sides of the handle bars.

Dad's girlfriend, Lois, didn't look too pleased when I turned up again at their house but it was agreed that I could stay. Dad made arrangements for my bed to be delivered and as it was only a two bedroom terrace house it was positioned tight up against the window of my toddler- half-sister's room. Lois was clearly not best pleased with this arrangement but at least she could take full advantage of my baby-sitting skills.

Mum was laying-out at the funeral parlour and the option was put forward to my sister and I to see her for one last time before the funeral. At first I decided against it although Carol called Dad and insisted she would go, considering it a good idea to see Mum at peace as opposed to the last memories she held of her in a distressed kind of comma. Dad's girlfriend expressed her opinion although I had not requested it. She said the idea of visiting a dead body was 'morbid.' I thought to myself what on earth it had to do with her anyway. After changing my mind several times on the subject I finally decided I would go and as Dad finished work I met up with him at the funeral parlour. Carol would go later-on with Christine, one of Mum's Littlewoods colleagues.

The receptionist welcomed us into the lobby area with a suitably sombre expression and a well-rehearsed speech. Something about being sorry for our loss and how peacefully Mum would rest now etcetera. After a few minutes wait we were invited through to the candle lit coffin area where I came face to face with the reality of Mum's dead body. I was ill prepared for the torrent of overwhelming emotions that hit me and with only a second or two of a glimpse of my mother's blue and white skin and dry ginger hair, I turned and ran out of the building it a terrible state of shock and despair. I didn't know how I would prepare myself for the days ahead of me.

It was to be the first funeral I'd ever attended and I didn't know what to expect or how I would cope. The little chapel sat in the middle of the large cemetery at Worcester crematorium. Carol and Dave entered and I followed behind them with my father behind me. The chapel was already full and as we entered the silent place everyone turned to look at us. There were no spare seats but someone had reserved a pew for us near the front. I recognised everyone's pale and shocked faces. Our old neighbours from Hollymount were all there along with our real aunts and uncles. Mum's friend Christine from work and even Lisa's mum had turned up with tears streaming down her face. Sarah wasn't there - deemed too young to witness such an occasion but her mother attended. Dad's emotional state was difficult to assess. Iris had left her makeup off and was white as a ghost. I suddenly felt sympathy for her and wanted to hug her but we'd never had that kind of relationship so I did not. Mum's boyfriend, John, had somehow managed to attend in a full black mourning suit. God knows how he'd explained things to his wife. He was totally distraught. It was the last time I ever saw him.

I'd never attended a church service before but we always had assembly every day at school. So I knew a lot of hymns although I didn't recognise the one that played. We all stood up as the vicar insisted and it was then that I noticed the coffin, it looked so small. Everyone ruffled their hymn sheets and my eyes rested on the words to the song that I did not know. And those that knew it had little strength in their throats to sing anyway.

'Abide with me fast falls the eventide'

'The darkness deepens Lord with me abide'

'When other helpers fail and comforts flee'

'Help of the helpless, oh, abide with me'

Watching my mum's coffin being lowered into the ground was a defining moment, a photograph in the memory that can never be erased. There was silence. There is no sound in the memory for that moment and only a picture of a wooden box in such a deep hole. There was the coffin with a brass plaque with the name and dates of my mother's short existence. She was only thirty eight. I stood, looking down and couldn't be moved. I was frozen to the spot. I was dead but still standing. It was horrific to know that she was inside the box and to cover it with mud and leave her there, unbelievably horrific. Billions of people have experienced that moment and will do in the future but that fact will never make it any easier for the ones who witness it.

I have no recollection of any wake at all. I don't

think there was one. I mean who would arrange it. Mum's boyfriend, John, lived with his wife who didn't know about Mum. Mum's brothers lived too far away. Dad lived with Mum's nemesis so it wouldn't happen at their house and Carol was only eighteen so unlikely for her and Dave to arrange a wake gathering at the council flat. I guess a few of the adults went to the pub opposite the cemetery or dispersed into several different pubs. I've no idea but I just went back to Dad's.

CHAPTER 14

Secret wedding

The very next day I was back at school. I'd already had two weeks off in between the death and the funeral. I was aware that the children were looking at me, checking for my reaction. They were twittering amongst themselves but not in a malicious way. The death of a parent was just something new and unimaginable for most of them and therefore a big topic for conversation. Sarah's mother had attended the funeral and she'd passed all the details of the day onto Sarah. Details of how I had stood over, 'staring down at the coffin.' How I had stood and couldn't be moved. How I was 'frozen with grief.' Sarah had relayed the details on to some of the school children and soon the whole of my class was buzzing with this information. One of the girls who'd heard it straight from the horse's mouth came up to check I was alright and she told me that Sarah had giving details of the story on to a group of them. She was disappointed with Sarah and so was I.

The following day and it was my turn to do the job of 'headmaster's assistant.' Every pupil in the fourth year of secondary school (i.e. year ten) was systematically taken off of the register one by one, day by day to do this functional job. Instead of lessons, whoever was on headmaster's assistant duty would spend the day sitting in a cold corridor just inside the external doors of the building and directly opposite the secretary's office. If any message or paperwork needed to be sent from the office to the headmaster or anywhere else in this large institution then it would be the child's job to do the running.

Luckily for me it was a warm day and so the vacuum of wind blew on to me as a pleasant breeze, as opposed to the majority of days that would not have been so kind. The hours passed with only one or two runs to do. Most of the time I sat in the corridor listening to the giggles of the secretaries as they did their paperwork and made their tea and jiggled the biscuit tin behind the closed doors of their office. I took my lunch break as usual back in the school hall that doubled as a canteen. In the afternoon I returned to my seat in the corridor where I rested with a glum face. The school was quiet and still except for the occasional teacher that popped out of class to have a break from the rabble and a quick chat with the office staff under the pretence of a certain random errand. Most paid little or no attention to me. But one female teacher actually spoke to me directly.

'Sorry to hear about your mum' she started.

'It's alright. 'This had become my automatic response. I had not yet learned that when someone says sorry in this context they are not apologizing for a mistake they've made, rather they're offering their sympathy and a better response might be 'thank you' as in thank you for your concern. The teacher stood looking at me.

'I suppose you think yourself very young at fifteen to have lost your mother?' With tears welling up in my eyes I looked up and nodded as she continued. 'Well you're not that young.'

With these words the teacher turned and left the corridor. As her loud footsteps echoed and got progressively quieter my inner turmoil spent far too much energy consumed by her throwaway comment. Perhaps she'd lost her mother at a younger age, perhaps at the age of five or six. Perhaps she'd not lost her mother but knew of someone else who had and maybe they were much younger than me. Maybe she hadn't lost her mother or known anyone younger than me who had. Perhaps she was just being mean. Why? Because it was easy enough to be mean. She had power and I had none.

A couple of months passed and I had not been to swimming club or taken a dance lesson. My ballet barre still lay idle on the floor of my bedroom back at the flat. Although at my dad's house I was now living closer to the dance studios near the city centre. So I felt the time was right for me to start again and I attempted to continue. My ballet teacher was pleased to see me at last and very sympathetic about my awful news. The lesson was hard as my muscles had weakened by lack of practise but most of all, my heart was so heavy that I struggled locating my kinaesthetic sense.

Back at Dad's house I felt out of place and awkward. His girlfriend, Lois and consequently my half-sister had been the cause of so much misery in my mum's last years of life and now I was shacked up with them. Also, she ran the house so differently to Mum and everything I was used to had changed. I kept getting reprimanded for the most minor of offences. When I used the hair dryer I had wound the wire up around the appliance as Mum always told me to do. But this was not how Lois did it and she complained to Dad about me and he moaned at me. I remembered next time and made sure I did it Lois's way.

They had a home telephone that I was not particularly interested in as I'd never lived in a house with one before. But their bill must have been abnormally large and they were accusing me of making sneaky calls without permission. If their bill was unusually high it was not due to me using it much but they were adamant and inserted a lock on the device to prevent me from running up the bill. This gave me a feeling of not being trusted, something I'd not felt before. On the rare occasion that I might like to phone a friend that also had a home telephone, I would have to ask for permission and if given, the lock would come off for a few minutes. I found this to be unnecessary and mean.

My father had no consideration for the fact that I was grief-stricken by my mother's death and refused to acknowledge the fact. As some kind of joke perhaps, he told me I should call his girlfriend 'Mum' now. I found this comment cruel and offensive and Lois wasn't impressed either.

I felt as though I was in their way and so I would often go to Archdale's club, in the evenings, to avoid them. I rapidly starting to become more and more interested in boys and craved their attention. Kissing and cuddling out in the grounds of the club with one or two different boys was becoming my drug.

There was a young man known as Eggy. He worked as a postman, at Worcester general post office, with my dad and Lois. He was a regular at the club and often said hello and was friendly to me. One Friday evening as I arrived at the club, Eggy came walking over towards me with a big smile on his face.

'Big day tomorrow en'it Jen?' I had no idea what he was talking about. 'It's the wedding! He continued. My face was blank and confused. 'Oh God,

Don't you know? Ya Dad's getting married tomorrow! His voice trailed off. He was clearly regretting letting the cat out of the bag.

Naturally Eggy had assumed I'd known. All the staff at the post office had been chatting about the upcoming wedding all week and passing their well wishes on to the happy couple and so when Eggy saw me it was instinctive for him to be excited and animated about it. Then his face turned white as the realisation hit him that I had not known. Now he might be in trouble with my dad, his boss, for informing me. I was confused and disappointed - what was this world I had come into.

Next day Dad and Lois went off to get married. I was not invited and their intention had been not to even tell me. They took Penny along with them and they were gone for a several hours. When they returned in high spirits I let them know I knew they'd married. I didn't know why they hadn't told me or invited me. I suppose it was all so awkward as Mum had only recently died. They could see I was upset and Dad looked at his new wife.

'See, I told you we should have told her.' He said.

Lois just nonchalantly shrugged her shoulders. Her face said, 'who cares?'

Within a couple of months of living at my father's house, his now wife had stopped talking to me and started to say that I'd done and said things that I did not say and do. And she was starting to stare at me, giving me that same look I'd first seen from her when she'd planted herself in the porch of my Hollymount house with the new-born baby. I had no idea why she was doing this at the time I was just confused but clearly she wanted me out. When she poached my dad from my mum she had not considered that my mum would die and she would end up with a distraught teenager in her happy home.

Sometimes to pass the time I would play with their record player or music centre. They were not accustomed to suffering teenage choices of music. So when my sixteenth birthday came up, they gave me a pair of quality headphones as my present, that way I could keep my music to myself. I was pleased with the gift but I pined for my mother.

On the evening of my sixteenth birthday I went to celebrate at Archdale's social club. Tommy, the guy that worked as a barman and had been fatherly towards me in the past by warning off Dave, knew it was my sixteenth (the legal age for sexual relationships) and was asking me for a kiss. So I stood on my tiptoes and kissed him on the cheek, he yanked me by the hips aggressively towards himself and insisted on a 'proper kiss' I pulled away from him, I was confused, perplexed and disgusted.

CHAPTER 15
Blizzard

It's a strange thing, how people who are suffering, attract one another like magnets. I was in the last year of school when a girl called Anna enrolled. She had long, thick auburn hair and she wore wide rimmed glasses that obscured her pretty face. She was originally from London and had an air of coolness about her that I aimed to emulate. She stood out from the crowed with her unusual taste in clothes and school shoes. I guessed she was highly fashionable in London but just weird by Worcester standards but she didn't care, she had a bit of the rebel about her. Her much older parents had apparently struggled to cope with her and had passed her on to live in Worcester with her older sister and brother in law. She hated living with them and missed London terribly.

A good friend was needed in my life more than ever and Anna filled part of the gaping void left by my mum's exit from the world. Anna was intelligent and hilariously funny, she was also streetwise but she'd learned this the hard way. She had a disturbing story to tell and because of this we were a comfort to each other.

One day she came to call for me at my dad's house. She knocked on the front door and he answered. 'Alright, I'm Anna - is Jenny in?' She asked politely, although in a cockney way. We didn't tend to start a sentence with 'Alright' especially to an adult but it was normal to her. Dad said nothing and left her standing on the doorstep as he came to get me from the bedroom.

'A girl called Anna's at the front door for you,' He announced.

'Great!' I said as I jumped up.

'I don't like her; I don't wanna see her here again.' He coldly continued.

I stared at him for a second with a perplexed expression. 'Ok we'll go out then' I simply replied. Then I ran downstairs eagerly to greet my friend, grabbing my shoes and jacket on the way.

'What's wrong with your dad?' Anna inquired, as we raced up the garden path together.

'No idea, what did you say to him?' I said.

'I just asked if you were in and ee just stared at me - like - gave me a dir'y look' Anna raised her hands, shrugged her shoulders and shook her head in confusion. She was at a loss to understand what she'd done to offend him.

'Oh well he's taken a dislike to you Anna, either that or he fancies ya!' I could hardly get the words out for laughing. I was so relieved to be out of the house.

'Oh leave it out!' Anna burst out laughing too.

She linked arms with me like she said they did in London. It wasn't a usual thing to do in Worcester but I was used to it by now. We laughed and joked all the way to her sister's house.

That was the only day Anna ever knocked on the front door of my dad's house. After that if she wanted to call for me she would come to the back yard fence and throw a small pebble up at my bedroom window to attract my attention. My bed was pushed right up against the window so I would immediately sit up and wave. Then I would grab my shoes and jacket and run out to her through the back yard, with the biggest smile on my face.

Anna was in the top set at school so we only had the opportunity to chat and laugh together during lunchtime and other breaks. Soon we were meeting up on the way to school in the mornings and then we were meeting up and not going to school at all. We would spend the school days in the town centre in and out of shops. One day we were hungry and had no money for lunch so we pinched some chocolate from a sweet shop. We got away with it easily and before we knew it we were stealing just for the buzz of it. The fear and subsequent relief of getting away with it and then the pleasure of having something new for free, was intoxicating and a great medicine for forgetting our troubles for a moment.

Christmas came and went at my dad's house. I was included in the family's festivities as they placed a Christmas stocking at the foot of my bed. The contents of which were nothing like the usual traditional stuff I'd have gotten from Mum but at least I was included. So I didn't know why I spent most of the day throwing up. I guess I just wanted to go home.

One snowy evening my dad and his new family were going for a night out at one of the working men's clubs we knew in Birmingham. I didn't want to go with them, preferring to visit Anna. Dad liked to be in control and didn't appreciate me having a mind of my own. He agreed for me to visit her and be back for my 11pm curfew. I had a key so I was free to let myself in to his house. They might not be back until the early hours of the next morning. So off I went, a walk of about a mile was not a big deal to me normally but in the snow it was a little harder.

Anna and I joked about and laughed together. She had a huge map of London on her bedroom wall and she pointed out the street name of her home address. She'd already marked it with pen-ink. She missed London so much, especially her friend

Geoff. There was nothing between them she said. They were just really good friends. She showed me a photograph of her and Geoff. It was taken in one of those photo booths and the quality was terrible. There was an orange curtain back drop and Geoff was so dark skinned that the photograph had blanked out all of his facial features. Anna's face was pale and her eyes were red from crying. It was taken on the day she'd been 'banished from London' she'd said. It had all been such an 'ordeal.' I handled the photograph carefully to have a look at Geoff and then we both burst out laughing. What a terrible photograph! We couldn't see him at all.

I left her house at about 10-15pm and by now the snow was frozen on the ground and a blizzard was picking up in intensity. An icy walk back and I was rushing to get into my dad's house and out of the cold. As I only had a key to the back door I went in through the back yard. I put my key in the door but it wouldn't turn in the lock. My hands were freezing as I tried several more times. It was no use; the back door had been bolted on the inside. I didn't know what to do. I was so cold. I struggled around the block of terrace houses to get to the front door but I knew it would be pointless. I didn't have a key to the front door and it was all locked up. I didn't know any of my dad's neighbours and by now it was 10-45pm and I didn't think it a good time to start introducing myself.

I struggled back around to the back door again. I don't know why really. Obviously the door was still going to be bolted. I started to feel myself getting choked up and as the tears started to roll, my face started to itch. All I could think of was to walk back to Anna's but it was at least a mile and by the time I would get there it would be way past 11pm and I thought I would be in trouble with Anna's family. I had no idea what time my dad and his family would be back and I just had no other option.

I started to push myself through the blizzard not at all dressed correctly for these conditions in jeans and a thin, white, cotton jacket. I was crying and walking and crunching through the snowy ground and as I got about half way I became more afraid about tuning up at Anna's house after 11pm. By now my hands were itching and I tried to shove them inside my jeans pocket to warm them up as best I could. It was no use I would have to go back to my dad's house. Again I went in through the back yard gate and again I tried my key in the back door. It was still bolted and locked. I sat down in the snow exhausted and wept like a baby.

I may have stayed in that position for an hour and hadn't noticed that the living room lights had come on. Then I heard the door unlock and my dad telling me to come in.

'Next time maybe you'll do as I tell you Jen.' His cold tone lacked empathy. I went straight to bed.

Anna and I continued with our occasional days off school and trips into town. We didn't miss too many days from school but Anna's sister and my dad were soon notified of our unauthorised absences. The writing was on the wall that I would soon be turned out from my dad's house but I didn't realise it. We continued going into town after school and continued with our petty theft. I soon had a few new outfits in my wardrobe, that I hadn't paid for. I never wore any of them; I don't think I'd acquired them for wearing. I didn't know why I'd taken them.

One time I came in as usual through the back yard. The washing was hanged there and I noticed that one of my pink, ballet leg-warmers was hanging on the line but the other one had fallen on the ground. I picked up the one that'd fallen and as I did so I noticed Lois watching me through the back window. I felt an eeriness and a moment of cold fear. She was standing bolt upright just staring at me through the window. I continued by taking the legwarmer into the house. It'd been on the ground and would need washing again. I explained to Lois about how the leg warmer had fallen down. She acknowledged what I said and told me to put it back in the bathroom wash basket. This I did. Later that evening my dad had a word with me.

'Lois told me what you did' he started. 'She told me she saw you come in through the back yard, you aggressively yanked one of your leg warmers off the washing line, rubbed it in the ground to make it dirty and then came and told her it had fallen off the line!'

'What! Why would I do that! Why would she say that? I was totally bemused.

'Well, she saw you, she was watching you from the back window.' He continued like he had evidence or proof that whatever she'd told him had to be true.

'I don't understand, why would I do that! Why would I dirty my own leg-warmer? I wanted to scream with frustration.

'I don't know, you tell me? You didn't know she was watching and she saw you come in through the back gate, you pulled the leg warmer off the line and rubbed it in the ground to make it dirty and then you gave it to her and told her to wash it!' he continued.

Lois stood looking at me with an expression like she had a heart of stone. I gave her a look of utter incomprehension.

'I don't know what's happening!' I felt like my head was going to burst. I looked down at the ground and walked out of the room. I made my way to the bedroom but that felt like no place of sanctuary. I rocked myself back and forth as I sat on the bed.

'Why, why, why' I repeated to myself. But no answer came.

I kept a diary in which I'd confided my feelings about my mother's death, my misery at living at my dad's house and how I'd been stealing from shops. Mum had always taught me to never read someone else's diary without their permission and I'd just blindly trusted that everyone else had the same rule. So, I'd never made any attempt to hide the book.

A few days later, I came into the house and found Dad standing in front of a black bin-liner full of 'confiscated stolen items,' and he was accusing me of being a thief. At first, in a blind panic, I denied that I'd stolen from shops but it became futile when he pulled my diary out of his inside pocket. 'Lois has read this and shown me you're a thief.'

The evidence was now clearly in front of me so I admitted to my crime. But my first reaction was to deny it. So therefore, I was not only a thief but also a liar.

Lois wouldn't have a thief and a liar in the house and the fact that I'd called her a 'bitch' in one of my diary entries hadn't helped either. The stollen items were being confiscated and I was to pack my belongings ready for my departure.

I'd lived at my dad's house for seven months and now it was time to leave. It was January 1981, I checked I had all my things that I'd taken there in the first place. Some of my legitimate items had disappeared as Lois had decided they were stolen too and they'd gone into the confiscated bag. The headphones that I'd been given as my sixteenth birthday present were to stay with their music centre, I had no equipment of my own to use them with anyway.

CHAPTER 16
The Evil

By now my sister was married and pregnant and Dave was constantly mean to her. Why she'd married him was a mystery. I could only surmise that she'd been bamboozled into it by Dave's pushy family and bereft by Mum's recent death she accepted easily under their pressure. Marriage to Carol gave Dave full rights to their now 'joint tenancy' of the council flat.

After loading Dad's car with my orange suitcase and a couple of boxes and bags I cycled on ahead. He would leave a few minutes later and meet me at the flat ready to unload my stuff.

On arrival at the flat I was all out of puff from cycling and dragging the bike up the stairwell. As Carol opened the door I pushed the front wheel in over the threshold.

'Hi ya' I spoke breathlessly.

'You ent bringing that bike in ere' Carol's said. 'You can leave it out on the stairwell.'

'It'll get nicked out there you know it will! I'll put it in me bedroom' I insisted.

'It's already full up in there with all the baby stuff, you can either leave it out on the stairwell or take it back to Dad's - it's up to you' She went on.

'Well what use is it gonna be to me at Dad's house?' I said with an exasperated tone.

Carol shrugged her shoulders as I yanked and pulled the bike backwards and forwards to manoeuvre it back out of the entrance of the flat. I must have pulled it too hard and as it shot backwards the back wheel got jammed in the metal railings of the communal walkway directly behind me and I huffed and puffed. I looked up at Carol with a defeated expression. Then I yanked the bike again to release it from the railing. As I bumped it angrily down the internal steps Dad was bringing my boxes and bags up.

'Where you going?' He spat with surprise in his voice.

'I'm taking me bike back to yours, Carol says I can't leave it inside the flat and I ent risking it on the stairwell so I've got no choice but to leave it in your back yard.' I said with a frown.

'Well it's her flat she can do what she wants' he said.

I rolled my eyes and continued bouncing the bike down the last few steps. Then I pushed it past the communal dustbins and hanging washing area until I reached the road. There I mounted it and angrily peddled like the clappers of hell, all the way back to Dad's house. It only took a few minutes with a combination of physical fitness and raging anger.

The gate to Dad's back yard was about six foot high and I stopped with the bike held in between my thighs to try to reach the latch on the inside of it. I couldn't quite reach so I leaned the bike up against the wall so as I could stand up on my tip-toes and try again. Almost on pointe and at the very end of the tip of my fingers I could just about reach over and push the latch across to open the gate into the back yard.

Inside the yard I leaned my green bike up against a corner wall, out of the way of the main thorough-fare. Even though I knew Dad and Lois rarely used the rear entrance I thought it best to avoid getting on their nerves by leaving it out of their way. If Lois moaned at Dad about it he was sure to side with her and then I would have to risk it on the stairwell at the flats. I didn't want to lose it. Besides it being a gift from Mum it was a really useful way to get around town.

As I was confident I'd found the most sensible spot for my bike I left it in the back yard. I stood up on my tiptoes again to lock the gate. Then I commenced the long walk back to the flat which took around thirty five minutes at a fast pace.

Dad and Carol were chatting on the threshold of the flat when I got back.

'We were just saying how bad tempered you are' Carol started.

'We should've you sent away to a home for juvenile delinquents' Dad chimed in.

I just stared at them as I couldn't find any words to express myself.

Then Dad continued, 'You're a burden on society you are, you shouldn't be your poor sister's responsibility. You're just a burden to everyone.'

'Why don't you go and live with Uncle Brian,' Carol suggested. 'You've always got on with him; you know we haven't really got space here for you.'

'He lives in Birmingham!' I said, 'What about school? Anyway if he cared about me he would av offered by now. He obviously doesn't want me there'

'No one does' Dad said.

'That's a crap school anyway and what's the point in exam certificates, I never had any use for em and neither will you ave' Carol continued.

'Can I sort out me stuff' I said as I brushed past the two of them.

I was back in my room at the flat that had now been turned in to a nursery in anticipation of the new arrival. I'd left the majority of my stuff in my bedroom there, while living at Dad's house, but I set to arranging my returning belongings. Dad had made arrangements for my bed to go there and it'd already arrived. My single bed was positioned up against a wall on the opposite side of the room to the cot that was awaiting the arrival of Carol and Dave's baby.

I started to arrange my stuff into the wardrobe expecting to see my things there as I'd left them in the days after Mum had passed. But most of my belongings had been moved and the partially empty wardrobe now had a few second-hand baby grows and other baby items in their place. There was still space enough for my clothes that I'd brought back with me from Dad's house and I put a few items in and then suddenly stopped in my tracks. Where was my ballet dress that should always be hanged and covered in plastic for safe keeping? I checked the chest of draws and indeed they were filled with my belongings but there was no sign of the dress that Mum had hand-made for me. On further inspection several items appeared to be missing. I yanked open the bottom drawer of my chest of drawers in search of the little white box. I felt around under the clothes as I started to feel rising panic. Then I noticed a pile of my clothes in a heap in the corner of the room and I eagerly rummaged through it in a desperate bid to locate the jewellery box. Perhaps Carol or Dave had found it and put it somewhere for safe keeping. I tried to comfort my mind with this probability but my heart felt otherwise.

I marched straight to the living room where Dave was sitting. He was smoking a cigarette and tapping his foot to the latest radio music whist staring at his feet.

'Dave, Dave.' I repeated until he looked up.

'What' Dave said.

'I can't find me mum's engagement and wedding rings, they were in a little white box in me bottom drawer, d'ya know where they are?' I tried to sound vaguely polite and un-accusing.

'What?' Dave grunted.

'Me Mum's rings, they're not in with me stuff, d'ya know where they are?' I continued.

'Yeah, I've sold em' He blatantly admitted, 'and don't bother asking for the cash cause I've spent it.' He almost sounded proud of himself as he added, 'Ya mum won't be needing em anymore where she is.'

'How dare you!' I screamed as I started to shake with rage.

'Fuck off' he replied, 'We don't ave to ave you living ere with us ya know. That measly child benefit cheque won't even cover the cost of ya food. Ya dad better be giving us some cash if he thinks we're gonna suffer ya'

I knew what he was saying, that I needed to toe the line. I swallowed my anger, my disappointment and my grief. I pushed it down and calmly went back to the bedroom.

I hadn't even considered that my things wouldn't be safe at the flat. The white ballet dress that Mum had made for me had been given away to Dave's little sister to play dress up with and there was nothing I could do about it. Carol had gone through all our mum's belongings too and distributed her clothes to Dave's large family and friends that all lived in the vicinity. This may have been therapeutic for her but it was awful for me. Mum had worn a blue and white lumberjack jacket in the last couple of winters of her life and now Dave's brother had it. Every time I saw him wearing it out in the street it reminded me of who I'd lost.

I considered the possibility of reporting the theft of Mum's wedding and engagement rings to the police but I had no proof that Dave had taken them and although he'd happily admitted the theft to me, he would surely deny it to them. Anyway I would have nowhere to go if I went and got the law onto him. He would definitely not allow me to live at the flat with them and then what would I do.

I continued going to school but I was on the far side of town now and my ballet lessons became fewer and farther between at the time when I should have been working my hardest for entry into vocational school. On top of that my ballet-barre had never gone up on the wall at the flat since we first moved there and since returning I'd not seen it. I assumed it had been thrown out and the dustbin men had smashed it up or someone else now had some other use for it.

Upset by this thought I distracted myself at school. The cornet soloist in the school brass-band had left the school and therefore the position was waiting to be filled. There were six first cornets and one of us would be offered this prestigious position. I anticipated it would be me. I had music in my blood. I had played recorders and read music from the age of four and had an added advantage over the others. My dad was a trumpet player and in the past I'd received private lessons from him.

The gossip at band practise was all about how the likely candidate for soloist was me. Then the music teacher stood up and it was time for him to make the announcement. I was pleased to hear that the position was mine. I even received a new silver cornet, on loan from the school.

Sarah looked furious. At the end of the day, as I was leaving school with another girl, she overtook us. She looked over her shoulder at me and snarled. 'They only made you soloist because they felt sorry for you cause ya mum died!' She almost shouted. I could only shake my head in a stunned silence. The girl I was walking with said I should slap Sarah. At least I should have a go at her, shout at her or something. But I couldn't, I had no energy left for fighting.

Instead I would concentrate on the positive. It was a poor school but it was famous for its brass-band and I was the soloist in the band. Sarah was just being mean as she was so disappointed. I would never excuse her for it although I did appreciate that she had no comprehension of my life. How would she understand what I'd been through? She was still living in Hollymount and that equalled Stability Street. At this moment in time, failing to make it to soloist was probably the worst thing she'd ever gone through. I should appreciate this and put it behind me.

I was miserable at the flat with Carol and Dave and spent as little time there as possible. If I had no clear plan for the day I would spend hours walking aimlessly around the streets of Worcester. It was on one of these days that a woman approached me. As a guess I would say she was in her late twenties. She had dark straight hair and wide rimmed glasses. Her manner was gentle as she asked me if I liked cosmetics and if I'd like to partake in 'a kind of makeup survey.' She had a few sample products in her car and could give me some just for taking part.

At any other moment of my life prior to that

day I might have refused such company. But I was sixteen and traumatised by recent events. Just to have a kind woman's face and a voice that sounded concerned and interested in me was appealing and I soon complied with her offer to sit in her car to avoid the blustery air.

In the shelter of her vehicle she asked more questions but she seemed less interested in my opinions on makeup and more interested in me as a person and my life, my family. I soon opened up to her and told her of my mum's recent death to cancer and how I was now being shunted from place to place with little hope in life and a feeling that no one cared too much about me. My voice broke as I explained that my dream of becoming a ballerina was starting to slip away. Her kindness and interest in me was intoxicating and I was candid and honest about myself.

'So you have no one then really?' She asked, 'no one would really miss you or notice if you were gone from here?'

At first I agreed and continued talking but then suddenly, as if waking from a drunken stupor, a pronounced sense of crises overcame me and an urge to get out of the car immediately. I felt almost ready to faint with panic, so vivid was my sense of crisis. Still I tried to appear calm and polite.

'Oh me big sister's meeting me ere in a minute, I

think I can see her, yeah there she is.' I pointed and waved frantically to a random female who looked perplexed as she walked in our direction. A cold glare came into the eye of the woman sitting next to me as she hesitated for a moment and then the door clicked and she simply said 'get out.'

Although the thought of suicide had previously crossed my mind, something in my survival instinct had forced me to escape the car that day. I was confused and unsure about my feelings but something had convinced me I was in danger. But I soon put it all out of my head. I had the constant threat of homelessness hanging over me to keep my mind otherwise occupied.

Worcester wasn't famous for much in particular. Of course there was the porcelain factory in the centre of town where they produced exquisitely decorated, fine bone china. Something that I'd never really come into contact with. Then there was the Worcestershire sauce factory that was on our side of the city. As a younger child it seemed a magical place where no one went in and no one came out, just like Charlie's chocolate factory! But then, back then, I'd also believed in Father Christmas.

Recently my city had become famous for 'the missing girls.' Carol-Ann Cooper had attended my sister's school and her disappearance at the age of fifteen, had cast a shadow over us for five years already. The local's thought she'd run away from her children's home with a boyfriend. We were blissfully unaware that she'd been imprisoned and was being held captive in a cellar under a Gloucestershire house. Carol-Ann, along with ten other young females, had been somehow tricked into going to that place. It was many years before their butchered bodies were found.

Perhaps I was the only one who knew how the evil married couple achieved these abductions. I was the lucky one who'd learned that Mrs West did Mr West's ground work. It was she who had an eye for the vulnerable, the broken-hearted, the homeless. It was she who entrapped them with her fake motherly-kindness. I recognised her on the news but that was over a decade after the 'makeup survey day' when the human remains were located.

There was a false sense of security around females in those days and we'd only really been warned of male snatchers. I had the image of a scruffy lone man probably dressed in brown and sporting a shabby beard. He would offer sweets and I was to run as he tried to grab me. In no way did this resemble the genius of the West's evil abduction technique.

CHAPTER 17

Love

I was living a lost and confused existence. My mind was like a perfect graveyard of buried hopes and dreams. Being unreligious and without a caring guardian I had zero resources to meet my bereavements, nothing except my own resentful will. It was as if the prodding spear of pain in me had left me no respite for judgement or sanity and I fell repeatedly into the eye of each coming storm.

One Saturday afternoon my friend Anna and I took a bus to Birmingham shopping centre. Not to steal anything, we'd both been in trouble for that and wouldn't consider doing it again. We just went for a day out in what I thought was the big city. We wandered around the Bull-ring shopping centre wide eyed at the huge array of shops and department stores. We rode up and down the escalators enjoying our big day out. As we came down yet another escalator we noticed a couple of older teenage boys were following us and we giggled to ourselves. Soon the boys caught up with us and introduced themselves.

Dennis was two years older than me. He was very different to anyone I'd met before. He was really into fashion and music. His way of dressing was stylish and he was crazy about the latest new pop-groups I'd not yet heard of. He was tall and really good looking and he was full of self-confidence. His Birmingham accent was strangely endearing to me and I was captured by his spell. As I had no telephone number at the flat he gave me his number and I said I would contact him when I got back to Worcester.

That evening I thought about Dennis. He was just what I needed, my own boyfriend, someone who would care about me. We might fall in love, get married and get a home together. With him in my life I could do anything. I could be strong. I felt full of confidence now and I had a more positive outlook on life than I'd had in a while. My young mind and body was full of hormones and my spirit was uplifted. I couldn't wait to see him again.

Next day I called Dennis from the telephone box, he was equally as keen to hear my voice. We chatted and flirted with each other and he asked when I would next come to Birmingham.

The following Saturday I convinced Anna to accompany me again. Dennis and his friend were there to meet us as we got off the bus. We held hands and kissed and cuddled and enjoyed one another's company while Anna chatted with his friend. That week I telephoned Dennis as often as I could find coins for. I was crazy about him and couldn't wait to see him again.

The following Saturday I was invited to Dennis's house to meet his mum, step-dad and younger brother and I could sleep over there. Dennis met me in Birmingham city centre and we went to a burger bar and held hands across the table. I thought he was stunningly handsome and I was infatuated by everything about him.

Then we took a bus to Dennis's little house and I met his family who seemed really nice and welcoming. His step-dad made us beans on toast for our dinner and we kissed and cuddled in front of the television while his parents were in the kitchen. When it came to bed time, Dennis showed me to his bedroom and made sure I was comfortable and then after some serious cuddling he said goodnight and went downstairs to sleep on the settee.

Next morning, Dennis woke me up with a cup of tea. A quick kiss and it was time for me to get up for breakfast. Downstairs at the kitchen table I chatted with Dennis's family a little whilst eating a piece of egg on toast. Next we were back on the bus to the centre of Birmingham. Dennis was in no rush for me to leave him and so we went into the Bull-ring shopping centre where we'd first met.

We wandered around for a few hours and then it was time for me to get my bus back to Worcester. As I got on the bus I turned around to say goodbye to Dennis.

'I luv ya,' He suddenly said with his cute Birmingham accent. I floated all the way back to Worcester.

The following Saturday Dennis came to visit me in Worcester! I was thrilled and desperate to hug him. We held hands constantly as I showed him the sights. I was particularly proud of the Cathedral. I had done a project on the ancient building whilst at primary school and as Lisa and I had often spent rainy days in there when we were younger, I considered myself quite an expert on its history.

King John 'the bad king' was buried inside Worcester Cathedral. I showed Dennis the lying down statue on the King's tomb and explained how no one had wanted the King's dead body and so Worcester had been kind and agreed to take him. As the King was so bad, it was a concern that he might not make it to heaven and so Saint Oswald and Saint Wulstan had been buried alongside him for a better chance of entrance through the pearly gates. I wasn't sure this story was completely true but it is what I recalled from my primary school project.

Dennis seemed captivated by the story and by me

as he held on to my every word. As the evening drew in I thought it would be ok to invite him back to my current address, the flat. Dave was out and my sister was uninterested so before we knew it we were in bed together kissing and touching. I felt truly loved and beautiful and before the early morning sun was up in the sky, the inevitable had happened. I felt like I was walking on air and wanted to run around naked out in the grounds of the flats. I had found a drug that made me forget all of my troubles. I was convinced Dennis had found it too.

After a piece of toast, later that morning, Dennis needed to get back home to his mother. He was eighteen and old enough to stay out if he wished but his mum might be worried. So we held hands on the bus as I took him back into town and waved goodbye to each other as his bus departed for Birmingham.

Next day I went to the telephone box as usual. I couldn't wait to hear Dennis's voice but on this occasion he was not home. He was busy, out at the shops, his step-dad informed me. No problem, I would call back again tomorrow.

I was so looking forward to hearing Dennis's voice and I hurriedly ran along to the telephone box the following day. My heart missed a beat as I heard his voice saying 'hello.' I hastily pushed the coins into the pay-phone. But as the money went through the voice changed and his step-dad said Dennis wasn't home. I said I thought he'd answered but apparently that was not Dennis - that voice had been his younger brother.

I had no idea what'd happened. Why Dennis was always out when I called? He loved me I was sure of that because he'd told me so. And now that we had sealed our love I was sure I was in love with him too. There was no-one really to ask for advice on this subject. I had my girlfriends at school. But they were just sixteen year olds like me, working things out by trial and error. They advised that I should just keep calling him and I did but I was getting nowhere.

Back at what I now called, Carol and Dave's flat, Dave was busy abusing my sister who was now heavily pregnant and depressed. He thought himself the big man living with the two of us and spreading malicious lies that he was having us both.

One snowy day I was wondering about aimlessly and decided to visit my mum's grave. The cemetery in Worcester was huge and the snow had covered all the ground. She'd been dead for less than a year and her grave-stone was not yet erected. The rule was that a year must pass to wait for the ground to settle before the stone could go up. On a normal day I would have found the plot easily but on this day the snow was thick on the ground and I had nothing to navigate myself to the correct location. I searched and searched the deserted place. It was a bad idea to visit the grave-yard on a snowy day and no live people were there except me. After reading the other grave-stones and trying to decipher where my mum was, I started to become really disorientated and upset! Then I suddenly became terrified and started to howl out for my mum like a puppy lost in the Alaskan wilderness. I ran out of the cemetery in a state of panic and then slowly made my way back to the flat.

My room, at the flat, backed on to the community dustbin building and there was a way to climb up the bins to the first floor and force my bedroom window open from the outside. That night I was awoken by the sound of someone rummaging around near to me and in my half-awake state I was unsure if I was dreaming. But then Dave's hands were all over me and his beer-breath was on my cheek.

'I loves you Jen,' he whispered, 'I never wanted Carol, I only ever wanted you.' Dave's voice was next to me. By now I was wide awake and struck with horror!

'Get off me Dave!' I pleaded, 'Can you get out me room!'

'It ent your room no more, it's the baby's nursery.' He was still talking but I'd got his hands off of me at least.

My sister mustn't have got to sleep yet and she'd

obviously heard voices. Straight away she came to check on me. Dave quickly hid at the side of my bed as Carol opened my bedroom door. To avoid startling me she refrained from switching the light on. I thought she could see Dave and would realise what was going on.

'You sleep-talking Jen' Carol spoke softly.

I held my breath as I waited for her to notice Dave and for it all to kick off. But Carol's eyes hadn't adjusted yet and she hadn't noticed Dave crouching down on the far side of my single bed. As I hadn't replied she'd assumed I'd been sleep-talking and she gently reclosed the bedroom door leaving me shut in with Dave.

'Carol! Dave's in ere!' I shouted. She angrily re-entered the bedroom and immediately switched on the light. She looked straight at Dave.

'I don't care! She screamed, 'You can fucking ave er!' and she slammed the bedroom door shut, leaving Dave in the room with me! I immediately shot out of bed and called out to her to help me but she'd gone back to her bedroom, her light was off and she was unresponsive. Dave followed her in and I spent the rest of the night sitting on the living room settee in the dark. I was afraid to sleep and so I rocked myself back and forth to try to find some comfort.

The next morning Carol came to me with a cup of tea. She was heavily pregnant now and her huge belly protruded from her tiny skeleton. I was about to tell her exactly what had happened last night. I didn't want her thinking I'd invited Dave to my room. She waddled over and sat down on the settee, next to me.

'Dave wants you out Jen' she spoke before I had a chance to speak.

'What? But - I didn't do nothing wrong! I replied.

'I dunno Jen, he says you're a slag, you've gotta go' She continued.

'He must of come in through me winda, I was asleep and I got a shock when I heard someone in me room.' I explained.

I was struck by the total unfairness of the situation. Nothing stings so sharply as injustice. I didn't mention about Dave having his hands on me or about what he'd said. I didn't want to hurt Carol with those details. What would be the point in telling her? She might be jealous of me; she might go crazy at me or Dave. I wasn't really sure how she felt about him.

'I didn't do anything wrong!' I repeated with both of my hands cradling my head. 'I just don't know what to do! I don't know where to go Carol?'

She shrugged her shoulders and then a blank look came over her face and she stared into space.

It wasn't that I desperately wanted to stay with Carol and Dave, I just needed to have a roof over my head somewhere. The flat seemed more like home than anywhere else as I'd once lived there with my mum. Although I'd not really had long enough there before Mum died for it to really feel like home. It never felt homely like Hollymount - that was where I truly longed to be. But that life was over and I had to live somewhere. I didn't know what to do. I still had the phone number of Derek, the hospital social-worker. He'd once said that if I ever needed anything I was to call him. Surely this was as good a time as any.

CHAPTER 18

Social Services

Being fostered by a family was an option but there were no available families on the foster carers list, willing to take on a teenager, in the area. So Derek contacted my school in the hope that someone might agree to take me into their home. An allowance would be given to anyone who could find a space in their home and in their heart.

By the end of the school day I was informed that one mother had put herself forward for the job. Her daughter, Sharon Marsh, was in my school year. I knew three things about Sharon; she was the tallest girl in the school at about six foot, she was top of top set in every subject and one of the kindest pupils in the whole school. On being informed that I would be moving in with the Marsh family I also discovered that her parents were recently separated. Normally foster carers at this time had to be married couples but this mother was accepted without question due to the urgency of my predicament. I was unsure if she'd taken pity on me or just desperately needed the allowance money.

Mrs Marsh was a good woman but honestly she was ill equipped to take on an unrelated foster child. She had three children of her own, an eighteen year old son, a sixteen year old daughter - Sharon (same age as me) and a ten year old daughter. The children were all reeling from the recent separation of their parents and Mrs Marsh was not coping well with her brood. The last thing she really needed was another teenager, especially a bereft one. But at least she attempted to help me and I was grateful to her for that.

The Marsh family lived in a small three bedroom private house near to Archdale's club. Mrs Marsh was also a very tall woman, like Sharon, at around six foot in height and her eighteen-year-old son was taller still. Even the ten year old little sister was my height already. Fully grown now at 5ft 3, I was like a miniature in a stable full of race horses.

There was no spare bedroom available at the Marsh's house so I was to share with the two daughters. Mrs Marsh seemed a pleasant enough character but she went in with a strict approach from the offset. I was to be in every night by 8pm which meant I could no longer go to Archdale's although the club was so close it could be seen from the bedroom window.

I was not used to such rules and found the whole

set-up very disturbing. It was so uncomfortable being the unrelated foster child in a house full of related people. I was not one of the family and by now I was depressed, disturbed and disorientated. The feeling of awkwardness caused me to spend most of my time there sitting on my bed, the nearest place to any sense of feeling 'home.'

I dreaded being quizzed at school as the ripple effect caused more and more teachers and kids to find out that I was living with Sharon's family. Periodically I'd get questioned about it by those who'd heard only drips and drabs of my story. 'Why don't you live with your dad?' 'Why don't you live with your sister' 'Don't you have any cousins you can live with?' 'Can't you go back and live in Hollymount with Sarah's mum?'

My head was spinning. Sometimes I walked in the wrong direction when I came out of school as I forgot where I was living. Settling in with the Marsh family was impossible without some kind of support but Derek or the social services never once came to check on me and Mrs Marsh was left in the lurch. We needed support but there was none. When the family had their own quarrels I didn't know where to look. I felt awfully embarrassed and lost.

But there was one good thing. The Marsh house had a shed where I could keep my bike which meant that I would have some independence and perhaps I could even make it to ballet lessons again. I thought it best to call Dad's house rather than just turning up and taking my bike. I didn't want them seeing it missing and thinking it'd been stolen. So I went to the local telephone box and dialled his number.

'Hello' Lois said as she picked up the phone.

'Oh hi, it's Jen, I'm just letting you know I'm coming to pick up me bike either today or tomorrow'

'Well you'll be lucky' Lois said.

'What, what d'ya mean?' I stuttered with nerves and confusion.

'Your bike's been stolen, you shouldn't have left it here, it's been stolen.' She repeated with indifference.

It wasn't out of the question that an opportunistic thief might get into the back yard and take my bike. It was feasible, possible even likely but something in her tone told me she was lying. She even wanted me to know she was lying by her tone. She didn't care, she hated me. I guessed she'd always hated me and the moments of kindness where all fake. I didn't expect Dad to be involved with this deception regarding my bike - that would not be his style. Whatever he was, he was not the thieving kind. Whether she'd given my bike away as I'd suspected or it truly had been stolen was neither here nor there. There was no point in talking to Dad about it. He would believe

Lois without a question of doubt and she knew it. The only relevant facts now were that another one of Mum's gifts to me had disappeared, I would never see my green bike again and I was now permanently without wheels.

With a feeling of desperation and a need to feel a sense of belonging, that evening I went out to Archdale's club at seven thirty pm as the doors opened. I managed to get an older acquaintance to get me a couple of alcoholic drinks. Soon it was way past the eight pm foster house curfew and I was a little drunk.

I stumbled in at around eleven pm. Mrs Marsh was up waiting for me and it was clear that she was frustrated and pretty upset. She'd already realised taking me in was not really working out for her and her family. I knew I'd made a mistake. I slept there that night and in the morning Mrs Marsh gave me a handful of coins and told me to run along to the telephone box and to call the social worker. It was obvious that my foster home was terminated and I didn't want to remain there anyway.

Clutching Derek's telephone number on a piece of paper I made my way to the nearest pay-phone. On explaining to him that I was homeless again, these were his exact words.

'You know what Jennifer? No-one cares if a sixteen year old sleeps out on the street or not.' That was the last time I called the hospital social worker. I hated social workers after that.

While at the telephone box I decided to try to contact Dennis again. His mum was out a lot as she worked as a Carer in an old people's home. Every other weekend she needed to sleep there to take care of the old folks. On all the occasions I'd called she'd never answered the phone as she was very busy and this time was no different. His step-dad answered.

'Can I speak to Dennis please?' I spoke with bated breath. On recognising my voice Dennis's step-dad sounded really pleased to hear from me!

'Hi ya! How are ya?' He replied. I instantly felt relieved. Then crushing disappointment as I was informed that Dennis was out again and all I could do was leave yet another message which would be pointless. I had no phone for him to call me back on even if he wanted to. I didn't even have an address other than the phone box I was standing in. Dennis's step-dad must have heard the despair in my voice and took pity on me.

'Why don't you come up and stay with us at the weekend?' He announced. My heart leapt from misery to thrilled in a split second. I had been worried that Dennis was not in love with me anymore but obviously he was still keen to see me if his dad was inviting me to their home. Of course, I still had the pressing issue of having nowhere to live but knowing that I would be seeing my boy in a few days' time made the circumstances a whole lot more bearable. I was to call again on Friday to check and confirm my sleepover on Saturday. I didn't go back to the Marsh's house that day, instead I asked a school friend if I could sleep on her settee.

It's difficult to sofa-surf at sixteen. You're at the mercy of your peer's parents and if they know your predicament they invariably say 'no.' The best chance is if they don't know your situation and are consulted along these childish lines, 'Can Jenny stay for a sleepover?' This only works if they haven't heard your business through the grapevine. When Mum was alive I often stayed over with different friends and was welcome. Things were very different now as parents were concerned I might get too comfortable and become difficult to get rid of. This friend's mum agreed for me to stay for one night even though she'd heard I was homeless. She pointed her finger in my face and with a stern look she said, 'This is only for one night you understand? Just for tonight Ok?'

The news that Carol had given birth to a baby boy reached me a couple of days after the baby's arrival. Also the word on the street was out - that I was free to go back to live at the flat. In fact Carol and Dave both wanted me to go back and live with them. Unable to hesitate under my circumstances I awkwardly collected my orange case and a few bags from the Marsh's house. Preoccupied with my thoughts of Dennis and with a total distrust of Dave and even Carol, I returned yet again to their flat.

I arranged my belongings in any available spaces in the bedroom that was now filled with yet more second hand baby equipment. Carol was in a foul mood as she returned from the hospital and taught me how to sterilize the baby's bottles and how to prepare his milk. She was sore from the birth and even more uncomfortable as the nurses had bound her breasts to prevent the milk producing. She hadn't yet bonded with the baby but I took to him immediately which was a good thing as we were to be roommates.

When the tiny infant cried out that night I waited a while. Surely Carol or Dave would come to my room soon and see to him. I couldn't bear to hear him screaming. He sounded as though he would break if he were left for long. So after just a few minutes I took him out from the cot and comforted him with my body heat. No one came, so with the baby in the crook of my arm I migrated to the kitchen. There I shielded his eyes from the brightness of the harsh light while I tried to recall how to prepare his bottle. Surely Carol would notice I was up and get up soon. I checked the kitchen clock. It was 1am. I could hear movement 'thank goodness' someone was getting up. But no one came so I started to prepare the baby's bottle.

Suddenly Carol's bedroom door was flung open. I hoped Carol was coming to take over but it was Dave.

'Turn that fucking light off!' he said and with that he flicked a switch and I was plunged into darkness. Luckily I had already finished preparing the bottle and so I edged my way back to the bedroom. My eyes adjusted and with the lights from the communal area outside I could see well enough to bottle-feed the baby. Then I realised baby needed his nappy changing. I was no expert at this and felt sure I couldn't manage in the dark. As he stopped crying I placed him down in his cot. I hoped he'd be ok until morning.

When baby woke again an hour or two later I left him in his cot and closed the bedroom door to muffle his sound. That way I had the use of two hands and there was enough light in the kitchen coming in from the communal area to manage the task of preparing another bottle. My eyes adjusted quickly enough. Then I snuck into the living room and located the nappies in near darkness. Back in my room I realised that I could put the light on, it was duller than the kitchen light and further away from Carol and Dave's room. With the door closed it was unlikely to disturb them.

Within days I had this routine down to a tee. I was planning on spending a night away with Dennis though and I hoped the baby would be ok without me. What if he cried out and no one came to him.

What if Dave lost his temper with him? It didn't bear thinking about.

Dennis's step-Dad had told me to call back on the Friday night to check and confirm that I could spend the weekend at his house. Whatever the reason for Dennis to be unable to come to the telephone recently, at least I now knew that I'd see him again and I was thrilled. So I went along to the telephone box, with some coins. His step dad was clearly expecting my call and sounded really pleased to hear from me. He confirmed that I could stay at their house and that Dennis's mum would not be there as this would be a weekend that she had to stay with the old folks. Then he really confused me by saying Dennis was not going to be there this weekend either!

'Ya do know that when ya come up tomorrow, I'm gonna want to make luv to ya don't ya?' Words spoken not by Dennis but by his step-father! I was horrified and dumbstruck. A thousand things were going through my head. My heart started racing and my hands shaking. The telephone was beeping at me to put another coin in and was threatening to cut. I quickly blurted out that I had no more money to continue and let the call come to an abrupt end.

I walked for a while and then sat down on a park bench in confusion. I reached the conclusion that Dennis did not love me anymore or maybe he'd never loved me. I found that hard to believe and

kept imagining seeing his face on the day he'd said '
I luv ya' with his cute Birmingham accent but now
I was wondering had he really said, I'll av ya.' (I'll
have you) Maybe I'd misunderstood him or maybe
he did love me but he just didn't know that I was
calling him?

CHAPTER 19

Dying Swan

Turning up for ballet lessons was becoming more difficult. The less frequently I attended the more strenuous, each class I did attend, became. My lovely ballet teacher, Barbara, knew that I had some ability and that I had been obsessed with the ballet. Knowing of my mother's recent death she took pity on me and kindly offered for me to attend free ballet lessons as often as I liked. I was thankful and very grateful for this kind offer.

If it had been a couple of years previous to this time I would have taken Barbara up on every free lesson possible. But now I was losing my strength. My desire and passion for the ballet had been fatally interrupted. My ambition was deteriorating and I couldn't regain it. I was exhausted and I'd lost my drive. I was distracted and my dreams were slipping away. I had no one to help me with the applications and I'd missed all the deadlines for applying to vocational ballet schools for sixth form. The realisation that I would never be a professional ballerina had seeped into my soul.

As I left my last ballet lesson the music came on in my head. I could hear Tchaikovsky's Swan Lake, the dying Swan. It was on repeat and just kept playing over and over. I never said a proper good-bye to Barbara. I hadn't realised or intended that my last ballet lesson would indeed be my very last.

Around the same time I came to my last days of secondary school and I handed in the silver cornet that had been on loan to me from the music department. We fifth years were preparing for the 'Leavers disco' as all exams were over. I knew I'd done appallingly. Exams had not been a priority. Moving from place to place and making sure I had a roof over my head had been my main concern.

Since employment was scarce for school leavers the government had put into place the Youth Opportunities program for sixteen to nineteen year olds. The idea was that employers would give work experience and teach their trades to school-leavers in return for free labour. The employers would pay the young person directly and then claim back from the government what they'd paid out. Although I'd never expressed any interest in the hotel trade the school had made arrangements for me to take up a six month, live in, placement in a hotel in Malvern, about ten miles outside of the city of Worcester. This situation would kill two birds with one stone. Albeit for six months anyway I would have a job and somewhere to live.

During our last assembly, announcements were made to the whole school that I and several others had done so well in securing 'jobs' to go to. We were given a forced round of applause as if we'd achieved something and we all frowned at each other in confusion. Employers were receiving free labour in the hope that they would train school-leavers and give work experience. We'd done nothing to secure our positions and therefore deserved no praise or congratulations.

The final afternoon of school came and we fifth-year pupils (year 11) were enjoying the leavers disco in the common room. We were able to attend this day in non-school-uniform. I was surrounded by children I'd known most of my life. Some I was close to and others, like Sarah, who felt like a cousin but whom I'd never seen eye to eye with.

Julie (the girl who'd taken in my rabbit) was there and as usual she was being teased and laughed at. She'd always been picked upon at school. She was skinny and stunted in height and she smelled as though her clothes were never washed. She was probably underfed or even abused at home and sadly this caused the knock on effect of being shunned by her peers. No one wanted to befriend a smelly girl. But at least she had a permanent address.

Most of us wore jeans and tee shirts to the disco including me. Some of us added a little eye liner and lipstick. Julie wore her grey school skirt and what looked likely to be her father's pyjama shirt. The mean girls, in our year, sniggered openly and said out loud how she should work at a jumble sale for her upcoming employment. Julie was just ill equipped in every way and an absolute outcast.

What caused a stir was when one of the mean girls noticed that Julie was wearing a rabbit's foot around her neck on a piece of string. She wore it like a necklace, apparently for good luck. I didn't want to look at it but I was curious. Then I remembered my rabbit.

'Poor Flynn!' I muttered, under my breath.

The disco was now in full swing. Excited teenagers, thrilled to be having fun on their last day at school, were jumping around and dancing. A sad song came on near to the end of the evening,

'Life is a moment in space'

'When the dream is gone'

'It's a lonelier place.'

I didn't want to leave school; it was the only stable thing I had left. I missed my mother so much. My dream for being a dancer was over and I was now a bird without a song. And I couldn't understand what had happened to my Dennis. I didn't want to think about the rabbit's foot but the picture was too clear in my mind.

I sat down and tears started to pour from my eyes. The more I tried to stop them the more they came. Anna and another girl sat next to me looking concerned but no one knew what to say or do. And just like that, at the age of sixteen, my school days were over.

Back at the flat, Carol and the baby were out and Dave started being unusually pleasant towards me.

'How was your last day at school Jen?' he enquired.

'Oh, alright thanks Dave.' I replied.

'You'm off to Malvern soon ent ya?' he continued.

'Yeah, tomorrow,' I was unenthused.

'You know them small grave ornaments?' he enquired, completely changing the subject.

'Erm yeah' I answered, wondering where he was going with this.

'Well you can nick em off the graves and sell em for twenty quid each, that's what I'm gonna do.' He announced. He was looking rather proud of himself.

'Air Mum's got one a them grave ornaments.' I said. I didn't like this line of conversation at all.

'Well if she has, I'm avin it.' He replied.

'No you ent!' I said and it came out rather louder

than I'd intended.

I shook my head and swallowed the lump that was developing in my throat. I wasn't interested in his next reply. I didn't know if he was serious or just saying whatever he liked to upset me. The more I thought about it the more likely I thought it to be true. It wouldn't surprise me in the least for him to stoop so low as to steal grave ornaments and sell them if he could make a few quid out of it. I decided the conversation was over and I went to my room to pack up my stuff.

After packing my case I asked if it was ok if I took a bath. Dave had gone back to being pleasant again and said I could. I didn't take too many baths at the flat as I was aware that hot water needed paying for and they didn't have much money to pay the bills. Carol always said that if Dave didn't waste all the dole money and child benefit they'd have been able to manage to pay the bills without a problem. But he always did what he wanted with any cash and she always struggled.

I kept the bath water shallow so as not to use up too much hot water. I washed my hair quickly and went to my room wearing two towels, a large one around my body and a smaller one as a turban on my wet hair. I went straight to my bedroom and closed the door.

There was no lock and as soon as I closed the door it immediately reopened as Dave followed me in.

It seemed he wanted to continue our conversation. He'd gone back to being charming and polite so I didn't really know how to ask him to leave so that I could get dressed. He chatted away, asking me all about my last day of school and about the youth opportunities program. I chatted along with him and every now and then I'd mention that I needed to get dressed in the hope that he would leave without being offended. We were both standing up and as he was talking to me I realised that we had migrated across the room until I was pretty much backed into a corner.

Then, suddenly without warning, he put his hand up between my legs and I froze as he put his other hand in the small of my back. I shuffled back until I was up against the wardrobe. I held the towel tightly around me. He'd stopped talking and was eye to eye with me. I knew there was nothing I could say that he would take notice of. I could say 'no,' I could say 'stop it,' I could say 'please don't.' But I knew instinctively that he would not be interested in anything I had to say right now. I was thinking 'Maybe I could fight him?' He was not a particularly large bloke. He was around five foot eight and very skinny and I was pretty strong and physically fit. But I wouldn't want to fight him while I was naked and I was pretty sure the towels would soon fall off in a struggle. I knew my father was much stronger than me as a child so perhaps all men were able to physically hold me down.

Suddenly we heard keys jangling. Carol was on her way back into the flat. Dave quickly rubbed me in between the legs then he turned and quickly left me alone. I pulled my knickers and jeans on and dressed as quickly as anyone could possibly dress.

CHAPTER 20

The Hotel

Within twenty four hours of leaving school I was at my placement in the Thornton Hotel. A family run business in a pretty old building that looked like a small stately home, nestled in the beautiful Malvern Hills. This was to be my work place and home for the next six months. I was to learn all aspects of the hotel trade. I would be trained as Receptionist, Chamber maid, Waitress and Cook plus I would learn all about hotel management and accounts. The owners were to pay me seventeen pounds a week which they would claim back from the government so it would, in effect, cost the employer nothing. Seventeen pounds was a minuscule amount but I would have my own room in the hotel in a picturesque area of the country and all my meals were to be included.

Awkward and embarrassed on my arrival, I was shown to my accommodation. The main hotel was a prepossessing old building with wooden panelling on the walls and intricate palace style coving and decoration. I had my own box-room bedroom in the annex which was a kind of pre-fabricated building at the side of the hotel with a bleak-view of the car park.

After unpacking I reported straight to the kitchen in the main building where I immediately met Jane the Cook. She was a plain but pleasant enough lady in or around her late twenties. She had apparently been struggling with the workload on her own for some time and seemed genuinely pleased to make my acquaintance.

The kitchen was down in the basement of the hotel and it was there that I spent most of the rest of my first day, peeling potatoes. I was not very good at it and Jane was genuinely surprised by my lack of ability. She enquired as to if I had ever peeled potatoes before.

'Did your mother never teach you anything?' She said. She didn't know Mum had recently died.

I shook my head and tried to get on with it. Jane grabbed the potato and knife out of my hand and with great ease peeled several potatoes in less than a minute. She passed the knife back to me and I took another potato from a large sack and continued with trying to speed up as much as I could.

I was instructed to be up and ready to work in the kitchen at 7am the next morning. I was given an evening meal and I went to my room where I cried myself to sleep. I was lost. I was only about ten miles from the city of Worcester but it felt like I was a million miles away from everything I knew. I felt home sick but I didn't even know where I was homesick for anymore and it was already on my mind about where I would go when the placement was over. There was no guarantee Carol and Dave would have me back at their flat and what would I do if I had nowhere to go then. Of course I didn't really want to go back there but at the same time I knew the area, the people and it was much closer to feeling like home than this place.

Every day I set my alarm and got to the kitchen at seven in the morning. At the end of a week of potato peeling and washing up I was given my wage packet. I counted, only seven pounds! Without any authority in my voice at all, I asked the lady owner why I was not getting the seventeen pounds I'd been promised.

The lady owner's face was shaped like a large mouse. She reminded me of one of the characters from Beatrix Potter. She looked sweet but she was a hardened business woman and tough as old boots. She explained to me that ten pounds had been taken out of my wage to go towards my accommodation and meals, leaving me with seven. I didn't know if this was correct or not and the only way of checking was through her. Even if it was not true what could I do about it? Making complaints would not make for a better life at the Thornton Hotel. If I left where would I go? So with little choice in the matter, I accepted the deal.

On my day off I was invited to Mrs Mousy face's house a few streets away. I thought this was nice of her to invite me along with her twenty year old daughter - Karen. They knew that I didn't know anyone in Malvern and so I thought they must be somewhat kind. Their family home was a substantial property, detached and situated in a couple of acres of apple tree orchard. It was easily within walking distance of the Thornton but they needed to transport an industrial carpet cleaner with them so we went along by car. Karen sat in the front passenger seat and I rode in the back. On our arrival the two of them lifted the cleaner out from the boot of the car and took it in to the large porch of their house.

As soon as I stepped in to their house I could see how wealthy they were. Mrs Mousy-face and Karen removed their shoes in the entrance area and so I did as they did. Karen struggled on in; carrying the cleaner and I followed them through to a huge open-plan living area that was carpeted in a beautiful cream coloured shag-pile. The two of them sat down at some very expensive looking white leather settees and I went to sit down with them. As I almost reached a sitting position Mrs Mousy-face pointed over to the vacuum cleaner and I suddenly realised why I'd been invited. I stood to attention as they offered me a soft drink. I knocked it back while they sat and chatted away amongst themselves and drank their coffee.

I quietly placed my empty glass on the edge of their antique coffee table and negotiated the workings of the heavy cleaner. It was uncomplicated enough. Every once in a while they would stop and call out to me if I touched something in a wrong way while I was trying my best to vacuum thoroughly. When I was out of their sight they came out of their seats so as to be able to keep an eye on me and correct me if I did something not to their liking. The stairs and the upstairs of the house would need doing too of course and by the time I'd finished I was glad that I'd taken them up on the offer of the soft drink before I started. I'd built up a sweat and been at it for over an hour. First rule for cowboys, keep your horses watered.

After the vacuuming I was free to go and so I took a walk up-hill to see if I could find the ballet shop that I used to go to with my mother. I found it and stood peering through the window at the wonderful array of tutus, leotards and pointe shoes. It hadn't changed much. It was still my favourite shop. Excited children were going in and out of the place holding hands with their mothers while I stood and watched from the outside.

A couple of weeks passed and it was a quiet day in the hotel with only a handful of paying guests on site. The hotel owners had planned a family day out together. This was my opportunity to learn all about hotel reception. Karen was normally responsible for this position and so before the family's departure she explained to me what I should do. I was to answer the telephone with a polite voice and announce 'Thornton Hotel, can I help you?' The family were not expecting many telephone calls and by the time the new arrivals came in, later that day, the family would be back from their day trip to check them in. I was only to answer the telephone and write down messages. I was unlikely to know many answers to any questions so I should just politely ask the caller to call back later. This seemed simple enough but I was nervous.

I sat down at the reception desk with my pen and paper as the family went off for their day out. After an hour the telephone rang and I promptly answered the call and politely announced,

'Good Morning, Thornton Hotel, can I help you?'

The caller enquired about prices and I didn't want to make a mistake and give the wrong information so I kindly asked them to call back again later. Another hour or so passed and I popped to the toilet, this gave me a chance to stretch my legs. There was no one about. I didn't want to leave the reception unattended so I hurried back as quickly as I could. As I passed along the wooden panelled corridor I could hear the reception telephone ringing. This time the caller wanted to speak to one of the guests in one of the rooms. I looked at the switchboard. I had no idea how to work it and so I politely asked the caller to ring back again later.

A few hours passed and the family returned from their day trip. Karen and her mother came straight to check on how my day at reception had gone. I explained that I'd been unable to put a caller through to one of the guests as I didn't know how to use the switch-board and I'd asked one caller to call back later as I was unsure of the prices. Karen rolled her eyes in her mother's direction and then said I was free to go. As I went into the corridor I heard them muttering about how useless I was.

A couple of weeks later and a group of army men had come to stay in the hotel. In the evening as I passed by the hotel bar the, voice of Karen called out to me to come and help serve drinks to the young men. Mrs Mousy-face was sitting down in the lounge seating area with the squaddies and she was giggling and thoroughly enjoying herself. As I entered the bar the youngest of the men asked who I was and was promptly told I was the 'youth opportunities girl' and my name was not mentioned. Karen poured their pints and I waitressed them over to the table. Then I went back to the bar and took Karen and her mother's drinks to the table. I was about to leave when the youngest squaddie offered to buy me a drink. I looked over to Mousy-face and she gave me a nod of agreement. So I sat down next to the young squaddie as he patted the seat next to himself and Karen came over with the soft drink I'd ordered.

I was asked my name and told the names of the four army members. The one that'd invited me was named James who was nineteen. They were on their way to the army barracks somewhere down south and were stopping over in the hotel for just one night. James seemed very interested and gave me his full attention while he quizzed me about myself.

I was used to being ignored at the hotel and so this level of interest enticed me. It was nice to feel that someone was enjoying my company and we started to flirt with each other. A couple of drinks later and James was putting his arms around me while his friends joked with us all. Karen didn't look too happy though and after my third drink her mother leaned next to my ear and whispered that I was to stop fraternising with the guests. I said goodnight to everyone and scurried off to my room in the annex. I would see them all the next day anyway as there was to be a big celebration and party in the grounds of the hotel.

I'd been at the hotel for around a month but so far I'd not learned anything other than peeling potatoes, washing up and vacuuming. It was meant to be my day off but it was a special summer's day. It was the day of the Royal wedding of Prince Charles and Lady Diana Spencer. (It was also my sister's twentieth birthday) To mark this day of celebration the hotel would lay on a huge barbeque in the gardens of the hotel and all of the staff, friends of the family and hotels guests were invited. I was invited too but I would need to work the day at the same time. It sounded like it might be fun though and I started to look forward to it.

The tables were set up in the gardens in the morning while Jane and I were busy in the kitchen preparing sandwiches, salads and cakes to go with the huge array of marinated chicken and meats for the barbeque. Jane prepared everything while I ran backwards and forwards out to the garden tables with arms full of sandwiches, covered in film to keeps the flies off.

Suddenly one of the workers called out to me saying that there was a young man at reception who was asking for me. I should run along quickly as there was a lot to do and no time to lose. Who could it be? Dare I think that Dennis had found me? It was just about possible. Had he regretted avoiding my telephone calls and was he missing me after all. I thought it unlikely but I couldn't think that anyone else would have made the effort to visit on this day or any other day. I hurried through the kitchen, apologising to Jane for the interruption of my work. Quick as a flash I went along the wood panelled corridor and up the stairs that took me directly into the hotel reception.

I was perplexed to see Dave standing there with his goofy smile, grinning from ear to ear. I quickly directed him out of the main entrance of the hotel building, out of ear-shot of the receptionist, so that I could listen to his explanation as to why he'd come.

'I've paid me mate's petrol to come and pick you up' He was smiling but there was darkness behind his brown eyes. 'Quick get ya stuff, me mate's waiting!'

I was thrown in to a quandary. I didn't know why he'd gone to this effort of convincing a friend to come to get me. I'd had no contact with Carol or Dave for over a month by now nor had I had any contact with anyone else from Worcester.

'Oh no, I can't leave the hotel today, we're having a big garden party for the Royal wedding and I have to stay and help.' I explained.

'It's Carol's birthday today and we're all missing ya, we wants ya back. It'll be different this time, it'll all be so much better!' He said.

'I can't go today, I needs to work, I'll have a think about it all, I've got to go and help with the barbeque now.' I tried to rationalize.

It was clear that Dave was not going to accept this. He'd made an effort to locate the hotel and he'd come from Worcester to Malvern and he didn't intend this trip to be for nothing. Also he'd convinced and apparently paid a friend for petrol too.

'I'll pay something towards the petrol money?' I offered, my voice sounding a little desperate.

'You either goes and gets ya stuff now or you ent coming to live with us when this job finishes, you'll be homeless.' He insisted.

He was starting to look angry. I had the feeling he was going to make a scene. I knew that he'd caused my sister to lose her job at the café by scaring the manager and I became stressed at the thought that he would go into the garden and upset the staff and spoil the day for the guests.

It was my sister's birthday and she was missing me! Well it would be nice to be back in my home town. I was missing the baby. And maybe it would all be different this time.

I was put on the spot and had to make an instant decision. I didn't know what to do and was next to tears. My sixteen year old head was a scrabbled mess. I nodded and then ran around by the front of the hotel's main entrance. I hesitated there for a few seconds and then ran to the annex. This avoided me being seen by the staff who were busy in the kitchen and the rear gardens. Quick as I could I pulled my clothes out from the drawers and the single wardrobe. I pulled the battered orange case from under the bed and threw it wide open on top of the bed. I shoved the clothes into the case and clipped it closed. Then I opened a plastic bag and threw everything else into it. A quick check of the room and I was out. I left the key to the room on the pillow.

Dave and his friend were waiting in the car a little further away from the main entrance. As he saw me approach he got out of the car and grabbed the stuff from me and threw it in the boot. Next thing I was in the back seat and we were on our way back to Worcester. I felt confused. In one way I was happy to be going back to the city were I knew everyone but on the other hand I had been quite looking forward to the barbeque. I had the feeling that the Youth Opportunities programme was just free labour to the hotel owner and I would never learn anything but then again I'd only been there for a month and maybe next month I might have started to progress. Now I would never know.

I felt bad for the way I'd left the Thornton hotel but the other option would have been to cause a fuss and God knows what Dave might have done if I'd disobeyed him. I certainly would've had nowhere to live in a few months' time and I couldn't face that.

I watched out of the back window as the Malvern Hills got progressively smaller, wishing I'd been able to say goodbye to Jane. We'd worked together for over a month in the kitchen and I'd started to feel some attachment to her. I consoled myself with the reasoning that leaving without saying goodbye was better than the scene that could have occurred if I'd insisted on staying.

CHAPTER 21
Milk bottles

I squealed with joy as I was reunited with Carol and Dave's beautiful green eyed baby. He was already two months old and although I hadn't seen him for a month he seemed to recognise me. I dropped my bags and picked him up from his cot. I cuddled him and felt a moment of pure ecstasy.

My single bed was on one side of the bedroom and the baby's cot was on the other. During the night the baby would cry out for me to get up and make up his bottle. I normally woke two to three times and got up as quickly as I could to avoid the sound of the infant disturbing my sister or facing Dave's wrath.

It seemed it was my job to get up in the night and care for the infant. As long as I did it Carol didn't but she did take good care of the housework. The place was always clean and tidy with a place for everything and everything in its place. She and Dave had certainly put their stamp on the flat and busily made it their own. Every trace of our mum was gone like she'd never existed. Although the carpets and furnishings had been chosen by her, all of her personal stuff had disappeared. Carol had gotten rid of it all in the days after Mum had died. Perhaps that was the best way for Carol to grieve by obliterating any sign of Mum. It wouldn't have been my way.

I knew that Carol was clinically depressed. By now Dave was punishing her on a regular basis. One day while Dave was out I made her a cup of tea and put it on her bedside table. I tried to communicate with her but she would not speak and she would not move from her position on the bed.

I heard the baby crying, back in my room, so I left Carol and went to tend to him. He was crying out for love and attention. I cuddled him and kissed his sweet wet face and carried him through to my sister. She showed little interest in him and as I instinctively knew his nappy needed changing I took him to the living room and cleaned him up. By this time most mothers were using disposable nappies but they were expensive and so this baby had the old fashioned terry-cloth type with the safety-pins. I'd learned how to do it and I did it well. After changing the nappy I left the baby on the living room carpet and went to the kitchen and made up his bottle with the correct measurements of powdered milk. Quick as I could I went back to the living room and sat on the settee with the child in the crook of my arm. He guzzled on the milk bottle, I winded him and rocked him and soon he was asleep. I put him back in his cot in my bedroom and went to check on my sister.

The cup of tea was now lukewarm and untouched and still in the same position where I'd left it, next to Carol on her bedside table. She was not asleep but she was not moving and her face was stained with tears and fresh tears were falling. I tried to console her but she would not be consoled. I went back to the kitchen with the cold cup of tea and poured it down the sink. I made her a fresh one and placed it next to her again on the bedside table.

I knew that it was 'baby clinic day' and the child needed his check-up. So I told Carol that I would take him. Back in my room I dressed myself and then I picked up the baby and added a knitted cardigan to the grubby baby-grow he was already wearing. I shouted out that I was going off to the clinic but there was no response.

With the baby tightly squeezed against my left hip, I bounced the pram down the stairwell with my right hand. At the bottom of the stairs I placed Baby safely in the pram and covered him with a light blue blanket.

'It's ok, everything's alright Baby, we're going to baby clinic, yes we are, yes we are.' I cheerfully chatted to Baby.

At the clinic they weighed the baby and although

he was a little underweight all seemed to be in order. The nurse naturally thought I was Baby's mum but I explained that he was my sister's child and she seemed happy enough with that. No one seemed to care that I was the child's aunt and his mother was nowhere in sight.

Dave continued to be his usual self only meaner. He continued to row with my sister and say terrible things to the both of us. Such as threatening to desegregate our mother's grave and constantly threatening to throw me out of the flat for whatever reason took his fancy. By now he was apparently beating my sister and threatening to harm the baby too. I did my best to protect the baby by keeping him out of Dave's way. I took him out for walks in his pram and regularly took him to the clinic for his weekly check. I didn't mind when people naturally concluded he was mine. I was very proud of him.

One day when Dave had spent all the food money on cigarettes and beer as usual and the food cupboards were empty, he said that I was to go out with him to get some milk. I naturally assumed we were going to the local shops but his intention was to steal milk bottles from people's doorsteps. We walked about until Dave noticed a house with a freshly delivered bottle straight from the milk-float.

'Go and get it' he demanded. I shook my head. 'Go and get it or you're not coming back with us.' I hesitated for a moment and then ran up the garden path and grabbed the bottle. Immediately I heard a man's angry voice behind me. He was screaming and shouting at me to bring the milk back. I didn't even look over my shoulder I just kept running and Dave ran too. Then, when we felt we were safe from the angry man, Dave took the milk from me and looked over at another doorstep. I knew what I had to do. I grabbed the milk bottle and we ran again until we were in the next street.

We came to the wall that the flats backed on to; it was around eight foot high. The wall had been especially built up high to make it near impossible for people to climb over. I thought I couldn't climb it but Dave was saying I had to. He didn't want us walking back around by the houses where we'd taken the milk from. Ordinarily I would never have attempted to climb it.

'Get over it you silly bitch' he said, and he had his hands out for me to use as a step-up. I did as I was ordered and clambered to the top where I was told to wait. Balancing there Dave handed me the two milk bottles. He managed to get to the top of the wall and over and down on the other side. I reached over and dropped the first bottle as he held his hands up to take it from me. After he placed the first bottle down on the grass I carefully dropped the second one to him and then with trepidation I scraped my knees as I struggled down the other side of the wall.

I was relieved that the moment was over but I felt angry with Dave for making me do it. I hated him so much but I couldn't show it. I had to do what he said. I had offended him once and now he was King and my sister and I were his slaves with no one to rescue us.

I had the feeling my days were numbered at the flat, I recognised the tell-tale signs, my sister's irritation with me and that evil glint in Dave's eye.

One day Carol told me, 'You can't stay ere anymore Jen, Dave said you're too lazy.' It was time for me to go.

For some reason Dave's parents (i.e. Carol's parents in laws) had offered to have me though. I wondered why. Could it be that they'd taken pity? I knew that there were some kind people in this world so maybe I would fall on my feet this time.

CHAPTER 22

Lodging

Mum would have described Jean and Albert and the rest of the family as rough, if she'd known them. I never really knew what 'rough' meant but I was starting to understand. People who had swear words a plenty and readily entered into physical altercations if they even thought someone was crossing them. But rough people can still be kind people, can't they? They were Worcester through and through, coming from generations of Worcester fathers and mothers. Not to say that's a bad thing in itself but they were just very different to us in several ways.

I was to share a bedroom with Dave's two young sisters, Michelle aged ten and Joy aged four. Dave and his brother Mike carried my bed out of the flat and walked it up to his parent's council house.

A small section of Michelle's wardrobe had been cleared for me by pushing her clothes over to one end. A pile of unhanged clothes were on the floor of the wardrobe and I instantly spotted my ballet dress in amongst it all. I carefully picked it up by force of habit. It was no longer pure white, the netting was now closer to grey in colour and there were red and green patches of what appeared to be crayon on the ivory satin. The zip that my mum had lovingly sewn into place was broken. I gently folded the dress and put it back neatly on the pile of clothes at the foot of the cupboard.

At the age of sixteen my school days were over. I'd come straight out with next to no qualifications. Over my years at secondary school I'd gone from an A student to a D student. After that I'd failed to complete the Youth Opportunities Program and like so many others from my school year, I was now claiming benefits for the unemployed.

The deal, at my sister's parents in law, was that I could stay there with them as long as all of my benefit money was handed over to Dave's mother. This was an amount of £10.50. With no other option for a roof over my head I complied. I had no idea that I was in fact entitled to claim for this amount from the benefits office and extra for myself as I was lodging and these people were not related to me.

During all of my house moves I'd always kept in touch with my mum's brother, my uncle Brian. As I moved from place to place I would always inform my uncle, by letter, of my latest address and situation and he would always write back insisting that I should stay at my sister's or my father's or foster care or now my lodging address or anywhere else that I wrote him from. Anywhere I was staying at all seemed to be, in his opinion, the best place for me to be. He never offered for me to stay with him and his happy family in his huge detached house in the suburbs of Birmingham.

It turned out that Mum had written a Will over the course of the months before she died. There was capital left over from the sale of our old Hollymount house. Mum had spent a lot of it on having the council flat done up and fully furnishing it. A lot of the remainder of the capital went on the funeral, and the grave stone. And of the leftover my sister and I were to receive a couple of thousand pounds each but not until we were mature enough to spend it wisely. It was my mother's dying wish that this money would be used towards a deposit for us each to purchase a home one day in the future. Otherwise we would only receive our inheritance outright when we reached the age of thirty five!

This arrangement was supposed to steer Carol and I in the right direction with regard to how we spent the money. I assumed that my uncle had advised his sister as her health deteriorated. They must have decided between themselves that we girls could be easily taken advantage of. They assumed that we were likely to flitter this money away and so they took these measures to ensure a sensible outcome for the future of these funds. My uncle was left as trustee to this amount and he had invested it wisely, strictly adhering to his beloved sister's wishes. But due to my dire circumstances, by the time I'd started lodging, he'd encouraged me to open up a bank account so that he could send me a small sum of money each month from my inheritance. This was £25 per month. As my entire benefits money was paying for the cost of my lodging, I lived off of this monthly allowance and felt like a traitor for going against my mother's will.

I was given meals at my lodging address but their food was very different to what Mum had served us at home. I didn't mind the food. It was pie and chips, egg beans and chips or beef burger and chips. Every day it was something with chips. At home (before Mum had got ill) we'd generally been offered meat and vegetables or fish and vegetables and only had chips once a week on Fridays. Still, I ate the lot and after helping to clear the table I would walk down to the row of shops where some youths that I knew usually hanged around. I would go straight to the off-licence and buy a family size bag of sweets every day or sometimes, bizarrely I might get yet more chips from the chip shop. I don't know why, I doubt I was hungry. I guess it was some kind of comfort eating to cheer myself up. After being underweight for most of my life, unsurprisingly I started to gain weight until I could be described as chubby.

I hadn't seen Dad since leaving his house eight months ago. But on my seventeenth birthday in September, he surprised me by turning up at my lodging address, with a birthday-present. It was a huge box of expensive chocolates and some gold ear-rings. I just didn't know what to say to him. I was holding back the confused tears. I suppose I was angry and upset with him for not caring for me but at the same time I still loved him. But even if I could have articulated my feelings he wouldn't have listened. I knew he hated tears so I held them back and I just said 'thanks' and he left.

The evening of my seventeenth birthday was spent at Archdales. I knew just about everyone there and felt a sense of security and comfort from being in their company. Since I was no longer with Dennis I had many situations on the go with several boys who were interested in getting their hands on me. I had girlfriends there too and we would chat and have a laugh together.

Everyone looked forward to the Friday night Disco when there would be far less of the older generation about. There were two disc Jockeys; both aged eighteen, who ran the show together. I was good friends with Kev and the other one. The other one was in a relationship with a girl I'd known from school and she was apparently now pregnant with his twins! She was not the only one from my school-year either expecting or already mothers of small babies. With the absence of many other life opportunities, becoming a mother seemed as good a raison de'etre as anything else and I'd already considered this option myself. At seventeen I'd slipped through the almost non-existent safety net of the social services but if I was seventeen and pregnant I may have been taken care of for the sake of the baby. This was also a way to get a permanent council flat of my own and a purpose for my existence all at the same time.

I loved and adored my baby nephew and knew how to take care of him so surely I would make a great mother to my own child. I toyed with this idea. Where would I live if I was to become pregnant? I couldn't rely on my current accommodation lasting. What if the authorities did not take care of me? The thought of being pregnant and homeless terrified me. What if they took the baby from me? I would be in an even worse state of mind than I was already in. No-one would fight my corner. Folks, for some bizarre reason already referred to me as a troublesome teenager - although I was really troubled rather than troublesome.

The other girls I knew that were already 'expecting,' had mothers to help them through it. They had the comfort of their teenage bedrooms, in their parent's houses, where they'd lived all their lives. There they could wait for their confinement. They had parents who would fight the authorities until they would be given a council flat of their own. They would be supported during the birth and helped with the raising of their infants. No one would threaten them with taking their babies away. Ironically, being truly on the constant edge of literal homelessness I was less likely to be protected and housed by the council than those who already had a home. I was less in a position to be able to risk it. I had the feeling that if I were to become pregnant I would instantly be branded an unfit mother. I knew there were women who desperately longed to adopt a baby. I imagined the possibility that I would have my situation used against me.

Also I had spent too many years with great expectations for my life to totally give up now. All the ambition and years of training to be a dancer was still inside me maybe not actively but dormant, not dead and buried yet. Deliberately having a baby to try to solve my problems in life was not the option for me.

I knew I should try to find work but even getting an interview was almost unheard of for someone in my position. The West Midlands had one of the highest rates of unemployment and no one was interested in school-leavers with little work experience. I did go to one interview though. A Chambermaid was needed at a hotel in the city centre. As I'd been on the youth opportunities program at a hotel I was invited along for an interview when I telephoned through my enquiry about the position.

A lady in her sixties and another one aged around forty, sat directly opposite me at the interview.

'Have you had any experience of working as a Chambermaid?' The older one began.

I felt overwhelmed with nerves and simply replied, 'No' I looked around like a rabbit stunned by headlights.

'When you phoned in you said you'd completed a youth opportunities program in a hotel in Malvern, didn't you do any Chambermaid work there?' she continued with a distinct look of boredom.

'Oh I never finished the six months, I only done a month and I didn't get round to being a Chambermaid.' I said as my face started to flush with embarrassment.

The younger one sat up straighter in her chair and gave me an intense look. 'Why did you leave after only one month?'

My nerves started to get the better of me as I thought about how I would explain why I'd left the youth opportunities program. I couldn't tell them about Dave coming to get me. I couldn't even explain to myself why I'd left. I couldn't tell them all about my situation it was all so inappropriate.

'Erm, I don't know.' I whispered.

The two ladies rolled their eyes at each other. I didn't get the job.

My second Christmas without Mum was spent at my lodging address. (My first Christmas without her was just a blur of repeatedly throwing-up at Dad's house and grief.) I decided to use my monthly allowance to buy Christmas presents and where better to go for Christmas shopping than in Birmingham.

As school was now a thing of the past, my friend Anna had returned to her roots in London. So I decided to find enough confidence to travel and go around Birmingham alone. By now I was able to navigate myself to the bus and on to Birmingham. I'd been there a few times and I knew my way around the main shopping centre. Of course, my dear wish was that I might bump into Dennis and truth be known, this was my main reason for going there.

Traveling by public transport was not a problem for me. In fact I loved to travel. As I got my ticket and found a seat my heart leaped with excitement at the thought of Dennis. Several months had passed since we'd spent the night together. I knew there was a possibility that I might see him in Birmingham. It was a Saturday and as we'd first met on a Saturday, I'd realised that he was drawn to the city centre as a regular pastime. I still had hope that we'd be together again but then hope is a tease designed to prevent us accepting reality.

I arrived at the Bull-Ring shopping centre in Birmingham and wandered around all the old places that Dennis and I had visited together. If I didn't see him I could always telephone again but the thought of speaking to his step-dad concerned and embarrassed me. Also I could do without the disappointment of getting nowhere again. I continued to look around the shops but although the department stores were packed with Christmas shoppers, I felt alone.

I concluded that I had nothing left to lose. I went to a pay-phone inside the shopping centre and dialled Dennis's home number. I heard his step-dad's voice.

'Can I speak to Dennis please?' I spoke in a way that implied that I knew the answer would be negative.

'Is that you again, Worcester?' I thought it was a little strange to refer to me as 'Worcester' but I supposed by now he'd forgotten my name so I confirmed that it was me and asked again to speak to Dennis, this time with a quiver in my voice.

'You're not still pining for Dennis are ya? You do know that he doesn't want to be with you, don't ya? I answered in the affirmative. I suppose I'd always known, since our night together, well since the day after, when he'd stopped coming to the telephone. But now I really knew for sure that it was over. I ended the call as politely and quickly as possible. I knew this time that I would definitely never see Dennis again.

I had no enthusiasm for Christmas shopping after that and decided I didn't want to be in Birmingham anymore. Worcester was my hometown and I wanted to get back on the bus as quickly as possible. As I replaced the telephone receiver I headed straight out to the old bus garage. The area was packed and there was an air of Christmas excitement.

The festive lights were twinkling all around as I crossed the road at the pelican crossing and in amongst the crowd Dennis passed me! He didn't notice me though as he only had eyes for the girl on his arm. She was a little older than me and really fashionable like Dennis. She had short, cropped, dyed-blonde hair and she wore a tiny mini skirt of the latest style. They were holding hands and laughing and joking together. Dennis was looking at her in the same way he'd always looked at me. He had, what I thought was, the look of love in his eyes. He was pinching and poking her as they laughed and giggled and I was wracked with jealousy. My mouth hanged open as my heart crashed into my stomach. I stood in shock in the middle of the road for a few seconds as the young lovers passed. Then I made it to the opposite side of the road to the happy couple and I stood and watched them enjoying each other's company until they moved out of my sight.

The problem with a person having a lack of love is that they don't know what it looks like and it's easy for them to get tricked into seeing things that aren't there, I guessed that's what had happened to me. I'd convinced myself that Dennis had loved me but I'd obviously meant so little to him that he'd not even bothered to finish with me.

Dread can start as a small thing, so quiet that you pretend not to hear it. But it gets loud, so deafeningly loud that you just can't ignore it.

I'd not managed to purchase anything from my Christmas list during my day in Birmingham. So, on the following Monday, I went into Worcester city centre and got everything I needed. For the family I was lodging with, I bought a large tin of sweets and then I decided that one tin was not really enough for a family of five so I went back to the shop and purchased another tin. So I had two large tins of sweets for the family. Then for my sister, I purchased a selection box of chocolates. I bought Dave a pair of thick white socks; I knew white socks were his favourite. The most expensive gift was for the baby. I couldn't resist buying the cutest pair of soft baby slippers; they would be his first pair. I didn't get my father or his new family anything as, bar his surprise visit to me in September, I was no longer in contact with them.

On Christmas day morning I gave the two large tins of sweets to the family and they gave me my present which was a pair of black school socks of the poorest quality. They were meant to be over-the-knee socks and one was over the knee but the other was not. I politely said thank you and tried to appear grateful for this gift. I had already dropped off my sister's presents to her, Dave and the baby, the night before Christmas and now it was Christmas day so I could open the present from Carol and Dave. It was a small packet of sweets, in fact the same make as the two large tins I'd given out.

In the afternoon of Christmas day my sister came with the baby, to visit her parents in law.

'Thanks for the presents Jen; we never got ya much so e'are, have this two quid.' Carol said as she tried to shove two pound notes into the front of my jean's pocket.

'Oh thanks!' I replied. I had been really disappointed with the little packet of sweets from Carol and Dave and the crappy socks from Dave's parents. But I could see that Carol felt bad and was trying to make it better and I was pleased with the money. So I gave her and the baby a hug and a kiss.

'Buy ya-self something nice with that alright?' she insisted.

'Yeah thanks Carol, I will. Happy Christmas! I said. My spirits felt a little lifted.

'Happy Christmas Jen' She replied.

With that she kissed me on the cheek again and I kissed the baby again. She called out 'goodnight' to Jean and Albert and left to make her way back to the flat where Dave was waiting.

Less than an hour had passed and I was surprised to hear Carols voice in the house again.

'Jen I'm really sorry, Dave said I've gotta get that two quid back off ya.' Carol sounded distressed and genuinely sorry.

'What?' I was confused.

'I'm sorry Jen, please just give us back the money, Dave's going mad and he's got the baby! Just give us it back!' She insisted.

'Alright, oh, ok, hold on, there you go.' I stuttered as I handed back the two pound notes to her.

With that she turned and left. I watched her going down the path. She was almost running. She was clearly terrified of her husband. It was only Christmas day but for us Christmas was over.

New Year's Eve carried us into 1982. Since I had no school to go to anymore and I'd ceased to attend ballet lessons or swimming club for a while, I spent my days either indoors reading or walking about the streets, usually alone. I still went to Archdale's most evenings. I was good friends with Kev, the Friday night disc-jockey, and we would talk for ages at the club on the days when he was not working. He was a good guy but I never thought of him in a boyfriend way. We were just really good mates. He was like the brother I never had. I felt like he cared about me and seemed protective of me and maybe he fancied me too but he was so polite that he never made any moves. I guess he sensed I wasn't interested in that way.

Albert (my sister's father in law at the house where I was lodging) seemed to have a twinkle in his eye for me and regularly flirted with me behind his wife's back. One evening I was out at the local pub that was almost next door to Archdale's, with my good friend Kev. Albert was also there, having a pint with his two brothers. As Kev and I left the pub we acknowledged Albert and his brothers and they acknowledged us.

We walked in the direction of my lodging address and as we did we heard a car revving its engine and approaching us from behind. We soon realised it was Albert and his brothers. Both Kev and I turned around and waved at them in the car. Next thing the car came at us full speed and as it did it mounted the kerb. I jumped to one side and Kev jumped to the other. The car screeched to a halt and Albert got out with his brothers.

Kev was only eighteen and these men were all old enough to be his father but for some unknown reason they had it in for him. Kev and I tried to calm the situation by smiling and trying to joke with them but these men were in no mood for joking.

'Why ya sticking ya fingers up at us?' Albert screamed as he lunged at Kev. Kev was silent with shock.

'We never Alb honest we never, we only waved!' I insisted.

Albert turned to me, his breath stinking of alcohol, 'Don't stick up for him, I know you fancies him, You're just a little slag!' He shouted at me.

My heart was racing so fast as I looked at Kev. I guessed he felt the same. We just couldn't understand why Albert and his brothers had turned on us. They must have really thought Kevin had stuck his two fingers up at them. But surely they could tell by our reactions that this was not the case.

As the three brothers got back in their car Kev and I sighed a breath of relief and started to continue walking. We thought it was over but after driving off they reversed the car only to drive forward and mount the curb again at full speed driving directly at Kev. Now Kev was running for his life. He ran up a small embankment and in a blind panic jumped over a flimsy wooden fence that collapse as he mounted it. Kev's wrist was broken but he managed to get up and he kept running. The car could go no further and so it reversed and the three men drove off in a cloud of dust. I was left alone on the street, heart racing in confusion and shock. I didn't really know what had just happened.

I could not and did not want to go back to Albert's house now! I wandered around aimlessly for a while and then I knocked on the door of one of my school acquaintances and told her what had happened. The girl's mum let me use their telephone to speak to Jean (Albert's wife) and this is what she said to me as she heard my voice.

'Albert told me what you said to him, you called him a bastard!'

'I never Jean, honest I never!' I insisted.

'You calling my husband a liar?' Jean continued.

'No I'm not saying that but I never called him that.' I said.

'You're not living ere anymore - come and get your stuff out my house!' She shouted before slamming the phone down.

I spent the night on the acquaintance's settee.

CHAPTER 23

Homelessness

Next morning, still dazed and confused, I went to get my belongings from Jean and Albert's house. I was expecting to spend some awkward time packing up my things but as I walked up the garden path there was an abrupt opening of the front door and one orange case and a plastic carrier bag was thrown out to me. The family had been through my things and kept everything else they wanted and packed up the leftover stuff that they had no use for. I stood on the path not knowing which way to turn.

The only possible option was my sister's flat. 'You can't stay ere Jen.' Carol said, she looked down-trodden and hopeless. She was saying something about our mother's grave stone, how it had now been erected but they'd made a mistake at the cemetery and put the stone in the wrong place. There was no point in visiting the grave anymore as someone else was lying under the stone and not Mum. I didn't take too much notice of this story.

I thought perhaps Carol was losing her mind. I couldn't stay at the flat but I could leave my bags there while I worked out what to do next.

I took a bus into town with the intention of pleading with the council to help me. I knew the council was the place to go if you were truly homeless. After a long wait I finally got to the woman on reception and explained my predicament. She could see I was young and at seventeen, she said, I was too young to get a tenancy or even have my name go on the housing waiting list. She was very sorry but due to my age her hands were tied.

The Social Services! That must be the place to go. As I was not yet eighteen then I was not yet an adult. Therefore I was too young for the council housing list then obviously, as a child, the Social Services would have to put me into a children's home. I walked through the town centre to where I had remembered seeing a building with a sign for Social Services. I walked in and went to the lady on reception. After explaining my situation to the receptionist she told me to take a seat in the waiting area.

Soon I was called and taken into a side room with comfortable chairs. I explained everything to the social worker. How my parents had divorced and I'd lived with my mum and then she'd died and my dad didn't want me. She offered nothing but advice and her only advice was for me to go back to my Dad. I continued to insist that he would not have me and that he didn't want me and she laughed.

'Don't be so silly of course your dad wants you.' She said. It was clear that the Social Services were not going to help. Derek, the hospital social worker, had been right when he'd said nobody cared if I slept out on the streets.

I thought of my uncle in Birmingham. We were not very close but surely he would not allow his sister's child to be out on the streets. He had a large, detached, four bedroomed house in an expensive suburb of Birmingham. I didn't relish the idea of staying there as I knew no one in the area but I had exhausted all other options. I went to the telephone box directly outside the post office where my dad still worked. I rang my uncle Brian. His wife picked up the telephone and passed me over. I blurted out my desperate story. I told him how I had nowhere to go since I'd been thrown out of my lodging address.

'I'm gonna have ta come ta stay with you Brian, I've got nowhere ta go, I'm next to the station, I'm gonna get a ticket now and then I'll go and get me bags and I'll take the train up ta Birmingham'

'Erm I don't think that's a very good idea now you hold on a minute. Now I know your father won't have you, bloody useless he is but why not go back to your sister?' Brian said.

'She said No Brian, they won't let me stay there!

My voice was sounding desperate now.

'Now you listen very carefully to me Jennifer, you do not buy a ticket and you do not get on that train.' His voice was clear and precise. 'You understand what I'm saying? You do not come to Birmingham today.'

I had a grandfather living in rural Oxfordshire and another uncle in Buckinghamshire. They must have known of my plight through the grapevine yet they had not been forthcoming in offering any assistance and I wasn't about to start any further begging. The chances of me staying with any of them and the conditions being suitable for all those concerned were slim anyway. By now I had learned that at least.

At seventeen and without guidance I was incapable of knowing what to do next. I wandered around the city centre. The police! That's all I could think of now. I walked up the steps of the police station but I was too scared to go in. I'd never been in a police station before and had had nothing much to do with them but had been brought up to respect them. The only time I'd even spoken to a policeman was on the day Lisa and I had wasted police time when we'd seen a pigeon trapped in a house in Hollymount. We'd telephoned the police from the local phone-box. We'd made an emergency call because of a trapped pigeon in a house where we knew the owners were away on holiday. We couldn't stand to see the poor bird caught up in the net-curtains. So behind our Mother's backs we'd called the police out. We'd both been scolded for that. Now I was a little bit afraid of them and anyway I knew it was hopeless and they would not be able to help me.

I noticed the Army careers centre. There was a sign up calling for New-Recruits to come in and take the entrance test, 'Today.' Out of desperation I went in, gave my name and age and took the test immediately. I was shocked when the squaddie said my results showed I'd failed! Perhaps I'd been given the wrong test paper, perhaps I'd missed a section of questions out by mistake, or perhaps the squaddie had messed up the marking. Maybe their advertisement was not really aimed at girls and girls were automatically failed. Maybe I was just too stressed to think straight, I don't know. I've no idea how I'd managed to fail it. It couldn't have been that difficult. I was too ashamed to hang about and ask questions and walked out as quickly as I'd walked in.

I took the bus back to the council estate area of my sister's flat and Dave's parent's house. By now it was getting dark. I was on the street where the lady had talked to me about the makeup and encouraged me into her car. This was near to the row of shops where teenagers and young adults with nothing better to do would hang about. I knew most, if not all of these youths and so I hanged about with them too. I told them I had nowhere to go and that I would sleep out tonight in the doorway of the Chip-shop. Most of them didn't take this seriously but as night fell a couple of guys said they would stay with me. One of these was Eggy- the post man that had accidentally informed me about my father's wedding that time.

As it got darker and colder the majority of the youths went home for the night until only Eggy and one other young male accompanied me. Soon the temperature dropped and became so unbearable in the doorway of the Chip-shop that the other youth had had enough and went home leaving just Eggy and me. A little more time past and by 3 am on an early March morning, we were freezing and exhausted. Eggy could stand it no more but being a decent young man he would not leave me there alone either. After some deliberation he decided we would sleep at his house where he lived with his parents.

Eggy lived just around the corner from the Chip-shop. We went in quietly and he snuck upstairs and got some blankets and pillows and brought them into the living room. Eggy made a bed for me on the settee and his plan was to go to his own bed. But I pleaded with him not to leave me alone. So he made himself a bed on the floor next to me and we slept for a few hours.

I was awoken by some voices coming from the kitchen. Eggy's Mum was in there with Eggy and she was furious that he'd brought a girl home. It was obvious what she thought we'd been doing. Then the voices turned to whispers and I could just about hear them discussing my predicament. Next thing, the hatch door opened and a cup of tea was passed through to me. A few minutes later and a sandwich arrived. Eggy and his mum were very kind to me. But I couldn't stay there.

I went back to my sister's flat to get my bags. They'd not been meddled with; Dave knew I had nothing of any value left. I took my bags to a girl called Caroline, who lived in the flats opposite my sister. I pleaded with her to let me sleep on her settee for a night or two and she took pity and agreed that I could. I left my bags with Caroline and went directly to the telephone box.

Now school was over my friend Anna had gone back to live with her parents in Battersea, London. She'd not stayed with her parents back there for long though and was now living in a kind of flat in Gypsy Hill in south London with another girl. We'd managed to keep in touch via the telephone number of her best-friend Geoff. His parents had a home telephone and if I wanted to speak to Anna I could call him and make an appointment for a time when he would try to find Anna and get her back to his parent's house to receive my call. We'd been using this system, on occasion, over the last eight months, since school had done with us and in a fashion, the system had worked.

I would always confide in Anna how miserable

I was and how I was still moving from place to place. She would always say, "Come darn ta Landon" with her cockney accent and I would always say I could not.

I was afraid. London was a big city, so far away and an unknown entity. I knew no one there other than Anna and that made me feel very vulnerable and reliant on her. Worcester was my home and my security. I knew everyone here. But the security and stability was gone now. I had exhausted all the options of places to stay and no one would give me a home in my hometown. They would only put up with me for a while until a reason would come up to push me back out. I could not risk another night out on the streets in Worcester and Anna was actually asking me to come and stay with her. To have someone enthusiastically pleading with me to live with them was like the sound of an angel calling. It was something I could resist no longer.

I rang Geoff's telephone number and was lucky as Anna was there anyway, visiting her friend. It was nice to hear a voice that sounded animated to hear mine.

'When u coming darn ta Landon? She joked as usual.

'Can I come tomorrow?' I mumbled.

Anna instantly agreed and I left the telephone box and went back to where I'd left my bags at the flat of Caroline, opposite my sister's flat. Caroline was kind to let me squeeze in and stay on her settee that night. This was especially nice as she hardly knew me.

I had three large teddy-bears and the little one that I called Craig. I knew it would be silly to try to carry them along to London with my other luggage. I didn't want to leave any of my belongings with Carol and Dave so I asked Caroline if I could leave them at her flat. I hoped one day to come back and pick them up. I didn't have much left of what my mum had given to me and these teddies were precious to me because of that. They were irreplaceable. I knew Caroline's young children would most likely play with them. I'd always tried to keep them nice and clean. I insisted I would be back to collect them soon. But I never collected them.

I knew Anna's situation was not suitable for me and I was scared to death of what life had in store for me in the Capital. But beggars can't be choosers and any kind of roof over my head, even most likely a temporary one, was surely better than none at all.

CHAPTER 24

Porcelain City

Next day I picked up my little orange case and a couple of plastic carrier bags with my belongings. A few clothes, one pair of pointe shoes, one hard-back book called 'The Colourful world of Ballet,' five Royal academy of Dancing certificates, a pink eye shadow, one photograph of us as a happy family of four taken in Hollymount and a primary school work-book with my school project on Worcester Cathedral.

I took the bus into Worcester city centre. I didn't strike up any conversation with anyone, even though I knew several faces. I found a seat next to the window and took a good look around me on the way into town. The transport went past the cemetery where Mum was resting and I thought about what Carol had said about the grave-stones being muddled up. I thought about my life and how it was like a perfect graveyard of buried hopes and dreams.

Then the bus took me past the road that led down to my secondary school. I knew the streets like the back of my hand. I looked at the people and recognised so many as we sped down-hill on our way into town. This was my time to think and to put everything into perspective. I avoided eye contact with those I knew by choosing a seat at the back of the bus and resting my head on the side window. I had nothing left to say to anyone, any-more, anyway.

I thought about my sister. Why had she not cared about me? Why hadn't she got rid of Dave? She and I could have lived together at the flat as Mum must have planned. But I understood as well as she did, how difficult it was to get rid of Dave. When I'd had a brief relationship with him I'd struggled to escape his grasp and that was after only a month. In Carol's predicament it was near enough impos-sible. Now that they were married and had a child she was stuck. His close family and extended fam-ily were all around her guarding her every move. Of course she should never have married him, she should never have gone back to be with him in the days after Mum had died. He'd taken full ad-vantage of the fact that she was grief-stricken and he'd directed her and ordered her to do exactly what he wanted. He'd even convinced her to get all of her inheritance money bit by bit by getting her to write to Uncle Brian with requests for pay-ment for baby equipment and other 'necessities.'

As the trustee to Carol's inheritance it was difficult for Brian to refuse when her letters pleaded for money for the baby and within months her money was spent. But the child had little quality equipment or luxury and what he did have was second hand. It's not clear what Dave spent the money on. But it was clear that he was a vulture who fed on our dead souls and now Carol alone would be his prey.

I thought about my dad, why had he not taken care of me? Surely a father has the instinct to protect a teenage daughter. But his new wife had overridden this rule of nature by convincing him that I was a burden and a juvenile delinquent. My petty-theft from shops, when I'd lived at their house, had helped immensely with this hypothesis. The best kind of lies disguise themselves behind some truth. Left over time they would reinforce this theory of my delinquency and deviance to each-other and their daughter until the lines between the truth and fantasy were unnoticeable. There was some truth in it anyway. I had bunked off school and I had stolen from shops. And I had panicked and lied when first accused of my crime, making me not only a thief but also a liar. This seed of my badness, left unchecked, would conveniently grow in their minds.

Since Mum's death Carol and Dad's relationship was somehow back on track. Not in so far as he would ever protect her from Dave but they were at least on speaking terms again. When I'd been desperate for a place to stay he'd advised her that I was not her responsibility and that I was a 'burden on society.' She'd relayed to him the evidence of my useless school leaving certificate results and details of my failure to complete the youth opportunities program and stories of boyfriends and rejection were also explained adding further proof of my inappropriateness and evilness until I somehow became the devil herself.

I thought about my uncle, he had a lovely life in the rich suburbs of Birmingham and plenty of space to be able to accommodate me especially as his eldest son, my cousin, was already away studying physics at Cambridge University. But my uncle had been devastated by his sister's death and put the stability of himself, his wife and his own children before me. He and especially his wife wouldn't risk upsetting the good life any further and convinced themselves that I was not their responsibility. Which, strictly speaking, I was not. Even if I had gone to stay with them it was unlikely to have worked out anyway. I was already too disturbed and unsettled.

Further extended family must have heard of my misery but they'd not come forward with offers to accommodate me. Our lives in different cities, towns and villages, had never crossed that often and we didn't know each other well. It must be easier to turn a blind eye or a deaf ear under these conditions. They could simply say to themselves, 'She's her father's responsibility, not ours.'

I thought about good friends from Hollymount. I had thought of them as aunties and uncles once and they knew of my plight. Yet they'd not come forward even on the day when my school had put out a request for a foster family. The truth is, I was unrelated and certainly not their responsibility.

I was disappointed and felt let down by all of them. I could not imagine that I would ever forgive their neglect. I intended to leave my city and have nothing more to do with them all. I got off the bus and passed the general post office where my dad still worked. The train station was right next door to the large post office building. I took a look back over my shoulder as I walked into the train station and there he was, my Dad. He was probably on his way back to work as it was lunchtime. I hesitated as I watched him pass. Should I call out to him? Should I tell him of what I was planning to do? That I was going to take a train to London and never come back to live in Worcester again.

The door to the music shop was wide open with the latest tunes blaring out loud.

'Take your hands off me'

'I don't belong to you, you see'

'And take a look at my face for the last time'

'I never knew you, you never knew me'

'Say hello, goodbye'

Say hello and wave goodbye'

What was the point in calling out to my dad? I shook my head and looking down at my feet. I went into the train station.

'A half single to London please.' I couldn't afford a return, even at the child price. I was going to be in big trouble if Anna didn't turn up at Paddington station in London as I had no return ticket and not enough money to get back home, HOME, I didn't even know what that was anymore. Anyway no questions were asked and I waited on the platform for the train. I'd told no family member or Worcester friend that I was going to London.

As I waited on the platform in Worcester I thought of Penny, my half-sister. She would be nearly six years old by now. Would she remember me or had she forgotten how close we once were. I knew that she must have asked for me repeatedly after I left Dad's house but that had been more than a year ago already. I wondered what Dad and Lois might have said to her and how they'd explained my disappearance. How the truth would be twisted and edited to make her stop asking about me. I wondered if she would continue with her ballet lessons.

Carol's son had been like my own child but he was

still a baby, not even a year old yet. He would definitely not remember me now I was leaving.

The prevailing wind must have sent the aroma from Lee and Perrin's sauce factory in my direction and I instantly pictured Hollymount. In my mind's eye I walked downhill from our old house and passed the closed gates where no one went in and no one came out. I remembered how exciting that place was. The mysterious Worcestershire sauce factory. Wasn't it just like Charlie's Chocolate factory? No! It suddenly hit me that it was nothing like my childhood fantasy. There must have been another entrance! There must have been another gate where all the workers trudged in and out every day. The gate that I always passed on the Hollymount side must have been at the rear entrance. How stupid and childish I was to have thought of that place like some fluffy Disney story. The reality was much different and that place was not filled with Oompa Loompas happily singing and dancing but real men and women who probably hated the place.

I was drawn back into reality as the London train pushed cold air at me as it pulled up against the platform. It was time for me to say goodbye and head towards the big metropolis.

With no idea what to expect next I sat on the London bound train as it was preparing to leave the station. The Malvern Hills and Worcester Cathedral were close up now (in the city centre) and I stared at them, trying to take a permanent photograph in my mind to store and call upon whenever, just in case I never saw this scene again. I felt a tremor in my hands and I tried to feel comforted by fooling myself I would be back in a month if London life didn't work out. I wondered how bad it would have to be there for me to come back here. Returning to the porcelain city, where I'd been reduced to sleeping in a chip-shop door-way, seemed unlikely. The train was moving slowly now and picking up speed. I pressed my face up tightly against the window, as children do, to try to grab the last few seconds of the view, my favourite view of the hills and the spectacular Cathedral. In no time at all it was all out of sight but clear as anything in my mind's eye forever. The man sitting opposite frowned at me, maybe unsure if I was an adult or a child by the look of me and my behaviour. I tried to compose myself in a more dignified manner. One more look and the view had changed forever.

I closed my eyes and thought of how a life can change so easily. How readily it can all fall apart like delicate, shattered china. How it can all happen in such a short space of time under a certain set of circumstances. Worcester porcelain had a figurine of a little ballerina in a yellow tutu called 'Tuesday's child.' Full of grace it was. Full of Grace like me. I imagined it shattered into a thousand tiny pieces.

In my case there was no backup plan. My parents had moved away from their respected families so that we had no safety net to fall into if things fell apart. Times were changing and the wider community had become less accommodating. Christianity was weakened and families were less likely to give their children the security of church community or the strength that can come from a belief in God. As I was no longer a cute little child, yet still not an adult, there was a weakness in provision. The safety nets of immediate family, community, extended family and social services had all failed me and I'd slipped through.

I'd gone from happy normality to hopeless abnormality. The bubble wrapped candy floss had poison at its heart and now I was on my way to the capital. Like a piece of fresh meat thrown out to the Wolves.

Foot-note.

Genetics is a well-known subject but it may not be as well understood as we think. I'd lived and dreamed about the ballet so much so that I believe it was in my DNA. But due to my unfortunate circumstances and repeated house moves, I'd had to quit at sixteen. This was one of my biggest regrets.

Many years after the ending of this first book, I

had two children - a son and a daughter. Their education would be of paramount importance to me and I was delighted as my daughter made it through university. While my son satisfied my lost hopes and dreams by graduating from the Royal Ballet School and becoming a world famous ballet dancer.

Leading to book Number 2

Printed in Great Britain
by Amazon

59154320R00139